## "He'd be nothing without his daddy's money."

Gabby snorted and pushed the stroller to the trail once more. The words stabbed Dylan's heart. She could have been talking about him.

"Has he bothered you?"

"His attitude bothers me. Other than that, he's harmless." Her footstep faltered, but she adjusted her balance.

He'd have to take her word for it. But it was obvious she wasn't telling him the whole story. His spirits sank. Why *would* she confide in him?

He was merely the uncle she was being forced to deal with.

When they reached the end of the paved portion of the trail, they turned back. Gabby didn't want to tell him about her personal life. He got it.

Loneliness smacked him square in the middle.

He finally had a life worth sharing but no one to share it with.

He was playing at being an uncle, playing at being a cowboy, playing at being part of a small town. Something told him he was going to walk away from Rendezvous disappointed if he played at being important to Gabby.

**Jill Kemerer** writes novels with love, humor and faith. Besides spoiling her mini dachshund and keeping up with her busy kids, Jill reads stacks of books, lives for her morning coffee and gushes over fluffy animals. She resides in Ohio with her husband and two children. Jill loves connecting with readers, so please visit her website, jillkemerer.com, or contact her at PO Box 2802, Whitehouse, OH 43571.

### Books by Jill Kemerer

### Love Inspired

#### *Wyoming Sweethearts*

*Her Cowboy Till Christmas*
*The Cowboy's Secret*

#### *Wyoming Cowboys*

*The Rancher's Mistletoe Bride*
*Reunited with the Bull Rider*
*Wyoming Christmas Quadruplets*
*His Wyoming Baby Blessing*

*Small-Town Bachelor*
*Unexpected Family*
*Her Small-Town Romance*
*Yuletide Redemption*
*Hometown Hero's Redemption*

Visit the Author Profile page at Harlequin.com for more titles.

# The Cowboy's Secret

## Jill Kemerer

**LOVE INSPIRED**
INSPIRATIONAL ROMANCE

LOVE INSPIRED®
INSPIRATIONAL ROMANCE

Recycling programs
for this product may
not exist in your area.

ISBN-13: 978-1-335-48807-7

The Cowboy's Secret

Copyright © 2020 by Ripple Effect Press, LLC

This edition published by arrangement with Harlequin Books S.A.

For questions and comments about the quality of this book,
please contact us at CustomerService@Harlequin.com.

Love Inspired
22 Adelaide St. West, 40th Floor
Toronto, Ontario M5H 4E3, Canada
www.Harlequin.com

Printed in U.S.A.

Peace I leave with you, my peace I give unto you: not as the world giveth, give I unto you. Let not your heart be troubled, neither let it be afraid.

—*John* 14:27

To Debbie Hanna and Ronda Gieskin
for your friendship and laughter. Love you both!

# Chapter One

"You can't trust a cowboy." Gabby Stover typed instructions for housekeeping at the front desk of Mountain View Inn, the premier—and only—hotel in Rendezvous, Wyoming. Bright June sunshine streamed in through the large windows near the counter, but she kept her focus on the computer where it belonged. Her shift as the day manager would be over soon, and she still needed to check tomorrow's reservations and review her daily checklist.

"I'd give the cowboy outside a shot." Stella Boone, the new reception clerk, pretended to brush off her shoulder. "That hottie is definitely not from around here."

Gabby scrolled through the reservations, not bothering to glance out the window to catch a glimpse of the guy. She did *not* have time to indulge in Stella's uncanny radar for spotting attractive men. There was enough to deal with at the moment, especially since Babs O'Rourke, the inn's owner and Gabby's friend, had thrown down a bombshell this morning.

Was Babs really selling the place?

Gabby took a deep breath to relieve the sudden tightness in her chest. If the inn transferred to new owners, she'd more than likely no longer have a job. And she loved her job. She'd been working at the inn since she was nineteen years old. She was good at managing it—enjoyed meeting new people and sharing her enthusiasm about Rendezvous with them. It gave her pleasure to make sure they were comfortable. Plus it paid better than most jobs around here.

With the baby to think about, she needed every penny. Her niece, Phoebe, deserved a stable home and wonderful childhood—the opposite of what she and her sister, Allison, had endured.

"Do you think he's staying here?" Stella asked. "Maybe I can be his personal tour guide."

"I wouldn't get your hopes up." Gabby forced herself to speak in a pleasant tone. "Take it from me, cowboys are liars."

"That's a rotten thing to say, considering you're such good friends with Mason Fanning." Stella pulled a compact out of her purse and checked her appearance in the small mirror.

"First of all, this isn't the place to check your makeup. It's unprofessional." She tried to inject as much sternness as possible into her glare. "Second, Mason is a rancher, not a cowboy. There's a big difference."

"Sure. Big difference. Whatever you say." Stella fluffed her hair. "Does this mean Judd Wilson made it on your hot list, or is he more cowboy than rancher?"

Hot list? Gabby's eye began twitching uncontrollably. She'd hired Stella as a favor to the girl's sister, Nicole, who'd recently joined her support group and was due this summer with triplets. But Gabby's goodwill was quickly running out. As for Judd Wilson...the successful rancher was a looker, no denying it, but she had no romantic feelings for the man.

A shame. Judd was a good guy. But she was always attracted to the bad boys—the charmers in Stetsons with a twinkle in their eyes and snake oil on their tongues. Thankfully, she'd come a long way since the Carl debacle, and she had no intention of making a mistake of that magnitude again.

"Steer clear of cowboys, okay, Stella? It's for your own good."

"You sound as uptight as my sister. Ooh, he's coming in!" She tossed her blond hair over her shoulder and flashed her biggest smile.

Gabby had to refrain from rolling her eyes. Only then did she catch a glimpse of the man.

*Oh my.* Hottie didn't do him justice.

Her heartbeat thumped as her living, breathing cowboy fantasy-nightmare strode her way. He took off his hat, revealing short, messy black hair. She tried not to stare at his full lips, dark eyebrows and brown eyes. His shoulders were wide, hips slim, legs long. He wore jeans, cowboy boots and a black T-shirt. Flawless. Her knees trembled. She firmed her muscles.

This one was going to be trouble.

He stopped at the counter and exhaled as if something heavy was on his mind.

"May I help you?" Stella batted her eyelashes.

"I'm looking for Gabrielle Stover." Even his voice was perfection. Low with a slight rasp—a shiver rushed over her skin.

"You're looking at her." Gabby pasted on her most professional smile. "What can I help you with today?"

He frowned, pulling out a piece of paper from his back pocket. She forced herself to look away from his sinewy fingers to check the clock. In another hour she'd pick up Phoebe from Eden's place and kick off her Friday night with a pizza. Maybe this would be the weekend she'd coax her niece to crawl. At nine months old, Phoebe was scooting and pulling herself up to a standing position with help from the furniture, but she'd yet to crawl. If only Allison could see her daughter... Sudden emotion clogged Gabby's throat. Her little sister would have been a great mommy if she'd lived.

The cowboy handed her the paper he'd smoothed out. She began to read. Her stomach dropped, leaving her nauseous, reeling.

*Oh, please, no. No...*

The man standing before her was Phoebe's father!

"Stella, keep an eye on the front desk." Gabby rounded the counter and curtly motioned for the man to follow her. She led him down the hall to her private office and offered him a seat before practically collapsing into her own chair.

"You're here for the baby." Saying the words out loud ripped something from her soul. He was here to claim Phoebe. He was going to take her niece—Gabby's whole world, the baby she'd been raising as her own ever since Allison's heart attack.

"Are you okay?" He tilted his head, those brown eyes darkening with concern. "You look...ill."

Ill? Of course she was ill! This was what she'd feared from the day Allison first tried to contact him. Her sister's poor judgment had led to a one-night stand during a trip to Texas. Allison had tracked down the guy, Sam Pine, and had written several emails to let him know she was pregnant and keeping the baby. He'd never responded, nor did he seem to be on any social media sites. After Allison died, Gabby had tried to contact him, too. As a last resort, she'd mailed a letter to the only address she could find linked to his name, although she'd doubted it was current. That had been six months ago.

Unfortunately, a father had rights, and there was nothing she could do about it. He was the dad. She was merely the aunt.

"I'm…fine." She tried to compose herself. "So, Sam, I—"

"Sam?" It was his turn to look green. "I'm not Sam. Sam died. I thought you knew."

Sam died? Relief swept in. This guy wasn't the father! He wasn't taking Phoebe away!

Shame brought her back to the situation at hand. She couldn't celebrate the sad fact Phoebe's father was dead. The baby truly was an orphan. How horrible.

"No, I had no idea." She shook her head. "He never responded to any of Allison's emails or mine, after—" she licked her lips and pressed them together, willing her emotions back in place "—after Allison died."

"I'm sorry about your loss." He averted his eyes, then glanced up at her once more. "What happened?"

She opened her mouth to speak, but the words jammed in her throat. *Come on. Tell him the facts. Don't get emotional. You've gotten good at it.*

"Twelve hours after giving birth to Phoebe, Allison was asleep in her hospital room and had a heart attack."

His exhalation came out in a whoosh. "A heart attack?" He rubbed his cheek. "In the hospital? And she died? How could that have happened?"

The same questions she'd asked herself countless

times since getting the call from the hospital telling her that her sister was gone. A fresh gush of pain spilled down to her gut.

"The doctor told me her death was caused by a spontaneous coronary artery dissection." Her tone was brisk and no-nonsense, nothing like her current emotional state.

"What does that mean?" He looked genuinely distressed, and her outward calm faltered a bit at the sympathy in his expression.

"A tear formed in her heart. The flow of blood was blocked. They told me she passed quickly."

"And she had no prior heart problems?"

Gabby shook her head.

"So you're raising the baby."

"Yes." She lifted her chin, daring him to question her authority where Phoebe was concerned. Then it hit her—if this guy wasn't Sam… "Exactly who are you?"

"Dylan Kingsley. Sam's stepbrother." He extended his hand. She reluctantly shook it, and he could read every question running through her beautiful slate-gray eyes. Why was he here and how would his showing up affect her life? He'd prepared answers for both questions before arriving.

He wasn't going to lie to her—not exactly. He simply couldn't tell her the whole truth. Not until he was reasonably sure she was raising his niece with love and stability. Two things he'd been deprived of as a child.

Gabrielle Stover sure wasn't what he'd expected—but then, he hadn't known what to expect. The internet search he'd done on her hadn't given him much to go on besides age—twenty-seven, four years younger than him. She had no social media profiles. Neither did he. First impressions? She was professional and not happy to see him. But why would she be? She didn't know him.

"You're Phoebe's uncle." She leaned back in her chair, eyeing him with suspicion. Her chestnut brown hair rippled over her shoulders in soft waves. The white blouse and crisp black pants she wore hugged a curvy but trim figure, and gave her the authority of someone in charge.

"Yes." The instant he'd seen her in the hotel lobby, he'd been drawn to her. The blonde next to her with come-hither eyes had been safe, but Gabrielle? Not safe at all. She was his type, which meant she was all wrong for him. A beautiful, confident girl like her would want someone dependable, a man she could rely on. No one had depended on him in a long time. Not even his own father. Dad wouldn't have sold his company, King Energy, without a word to him if he had. Worst of all, though, Dylan had failed the one person who once upon a time *had* relied on him—Sam.

"Why are you here?" Gabrielle pierced him with a laser-like stare. He tried not to squirm.

"I want to meet my niece." Dylan planned on more than meeting the child. He intended to set up a trust fund for Phoebe and monthly child support, too. He could afford it. It was the least he could do for Sam's little girl. But he wasn't doing either until he knew for sure Gabrielle was raising the baby with love. And that meant keeping the fact he was a multimillionaire a secret.

What advice would his late father give in this situation? Dad would probably tell him not to screw it up.

Money had only bought him and his father trouble when it came to women.

At least Gabrielle would have to dig deep to find out Dylan was rich. He'd always gone by his middle name, and his father had been private to the point of almost being reclusive. The man never mentioned his son in the rare interviews he'd given. The first fifteen pages of results for Dylan Kingsley in any search engine displayed articles by an astrophysicist with the same name.

"Why now?" Cocking her head, she narrowed her eyes. "She's nine months old. Allison and I repeatedly tried to contact him until six months ago. Why are you showing up here after all this time?"

"I didn't know about the baby until last week." It was the truth. But at the skeptical gleam in her eyes, he continued. "Sam died over a year ago. My father had a stroke and passed not long after. I hit the road. When I came back to Texas last week, it was the first I knew of the baby. Your letter had been sent to my address. Sam lived with me briefly before moving to Austin."

"I'm sorry about your family." She had the grace to appear contrite. "How did Sam die?"

He flexed his jaw. Thinking about his brother always ripped him up inside. Almost nine years younger than Dylan, Sam had come into his life as a happy five-year-old when Dylan's mother married husband number three. Despite the age gap, Dylan and Sam had been close. And he'd let his little brother down. "Does it matter?"

Her eyes widened, lips parted to ask a question. He braced himself. But she didn't speak.

"He's gone, and he's not coming back." Dylan couldn't bring himself to tell a stranger that Sam had died of a drug overdose. He wouldn't let her think the worst about his brother. He still couldn't believe his brother had been messing around with heroin. Worse, Dylan had been wallowing in his own problems and hadn't taken Sam's call the week he'd died. Could he have stopped him from overdosing?

He'd always regret it.

"It matters to me." She leaned forward with her hands clasped on the desk. "I need to know Phoebe's health history. If he had cancer or diabetes or heart problems…"

Fair enough. She had a point.

"It was an overdose—an accidental overdose."

"Oh."

Right about now would be when he'd expect her to ask about Sam's estate—find out if Phoebe had inherited anything. His own mother would have dollar signs in her eyes in this situation. She'd used him to squeeze money out of his father countless times. And then there was Dylan's ex-girlfriend. Robin not only dumped him when his dad sold King Energy, but she'd also had the nerve to try to get back together after finding out he'd inherited Dad's fortune.

His niece would never be used as a pawn for money if he had anything to say about it.

"Were you close to him?" Gabrielle's tone softened, and sympathy brightened her face.

"Yes, I was." He hadn't expected sympathy.

"I was close to Allison, too." Her words broke at the end. "I miss her."

The naked emotion touched him. He missed Sam, too. To distract himself, he studied her office. Paneled walls, jewel-toned carpet, an oak desk and two typical conference room chairs. A file cabinet stood to the side, and a potted tree was in the corner. The walls had two framed paintings of mountain scenes. No personal photos he could see.

Doting moms usually splattered pictures of their kids all over their offices. Why weren't there any photos of the baby?

"So you work here, huh?" he said.

"I do. I'm the day manager." It was as though an iron curtain fell over her earlier vulnerability. She straightened, all brisk and no-nonsense. "What did you say you'd been doing for the past year?"

*Be careful what you say.* "Moving around. This and that…"

"I see." Disapproval radiated loud and clear through her pursed lips.

He doubted she did. Three days after his father's funeral, he'd packed his bags and flown to France. Two weeks later, he'd moved on to Italy, then Germany, the Alps, Finland and wherever the wind had taken him. He wished he could say he'd enjoyed the traveling, but it had underscored his new reality.

He was alone. He had no purpose. And no amount of money or traveling would change it.

"Can I see the baby?" he asked.

"My shift ends soon." She stood with her head high. "You can come over to my apartment around six to meet Phoebe."

Surprised, he rose. He hadn't expected her to allow him to see the baby so quickly.

"Here's my address. It's not far." She scribbled it on a piece of paper and handed it to him.

"Thanks." He slipped it into his back pocket.

She escorted him to the door, down the hall and back

to the front desk. She wasn't short, but he had at least six inches on her. She was a very attractive woman, reminding him of the fact he had to be careful where she was concerned. He couldn't let chemistry affect his ability to size up her parenting skills.

"I'll see you in a little while." He put his cowboy hat back on and nodded to her before exiting. With nothing else to do, he figured he'd drive through the small town. It would be good to get a feel for the community his niece would be growing up in. If all went well, he'd meet the baby tonight and be satisfied she was in good hands.

Since Gabrielle thought he was just some guy off the street, she wouldn't have any reason to put on a false motherly act to press him for money. If he got a sense of peace about her raising Phoebe, in the morning he'd tell her he was directing his attorney to set up the trust fund and child support. Then he'd...

A breeze caressed his face as he strode to the truck he'd rented.

What? What was he going to do next?

He didn't know. He'd been wandering without direction for a long time. A night in Rendezvous, Wyoming, wasn't going to cough up answers for him. He wished he knew what would.

"This visit isn't going to change anything." Gabby took Phoebe out of Eden's arms and kissed the baby's soft cheeks. Her giggles filled the small apartment Gabby called home. Eden Page was one of her best friends as well as Phoebe's babysitter. Gabby usually picked up Phoebe from Eden's, but today she'd asked her friend for a favor. "Thank you so much for bringing her over. I don't have much time to get this place in shape. It was so weird having him show up like that. At first I thought he was the father. But he's not. Sam died. He's Sam's stepbrother."

"He died?" Eden's expressive brown eyes oozed with compassion. "So Phoebe will never meet her daddy. That's so sad."

"I know. It is."

"And this uncle wants to meet her, huh?" Eden set the diaper bag on the foyer floor. "That's it?"

"Yes. At least that's what he said." She bit the right side of her bottom lip. "If he thinks I'm going to share custody with him, he's fooling himself."

"Did he say he wanted to?"

"No, but all the way home, I've been going through worst-case scenarios."

"Remember what Babs always tells you. Don't borrow trouble." Eden scanned the living room and shrugged. "Your place looks good to me. I'll give the kitchen a once-over if you'd like."

"Would you? Oh, you are a lifesaver!" Gabby set Phoebe on the quilted mat in the living room and handed her a toy while Eden crossed over to the kitchen separated from the living room by a counter with bar stools. "How did the week go without having Noah around?"

"I miss him. He's such a sweet little boy. But having all the one-on-one time with Phoebe is making up for it a little bit."

Until last week, Eden had also been babysitting her nephew, Noah. But now that her brother-in-law, Mason, had gotten remarried, he and his new wife, Brittany, were splitting childcare duties and didn't need Eden's

services anymore. Gabby envied Mason a tiny bit—
he'd found someone to share his life with. Part of her
wished she could have a relationship like theirs, too.
But it wasn't likely. She'd be the first to admit she had
trust issues when it came to men.

"Not having Noah around must be a big change for
you." Gabby tossed a few toys into a basket.

"It is, and I hate change. But I can't stop it." Eden
rinsed a mug. "By the way, I'm glad you invited this
guy—Dylan, right?—over to meet the little sweetie.
You wouldn't want to deprive her of an uncle."

"No, I couldn't deprive her of an uncle." A teeny
part of her *did* want to deprive Phoebe of this particular
one, though. If Dylan was anything like her own father
or Carl, she wanted her niece as far from him as possible. At the moment, she didn't see much difference
between him and them, but she wasn't being fair. She
didn't know him at all. "One thing's for sure—we're
going to have a *lot* to talk about at this week's meeting."

"When don't we?" Eden grinned.

Gabby, Eden, Mason and Nicole met every Tuesday
at the inn for their support group. They'd all lost loved
ones who'd been in the prime of their lives. Mason's
first wife, Mia, who was Eden's older sister, had died
of cancer six months after Noah was born. Gabby had
lost Allison last year and Nicole's husband died unex-
pectedly on Christmas Day due to complications from
muscular dystrophy.

Eden glanced up. "How long did you say he'd be in
town?"

"He didn't say. I doubt long." Keeping an eye on
Phoebe, Gabby tidied the magazines on the end table.
Dylan had drifter written all over him. If he'd been

moving around for a year, doing who knew what after his father died...

It didn't take much of a stretch of the imagination to figure out the guy didn't have a job, didn't have roots. Maybe he'd come into a small inheritance and rather than put it toward his future, he was running through it like a fool. Or he could be like her daddy, latching on to a new woman in each town to support him. Both scenarios spelled deadbeat. The muscles in her neck tightened.

"I'm fine with him meeting Phoebe, but I can tell you right now, I'm not going to have her influenced by some charming, shifty cowboy who will only let her down. If he wants to visit now and then, fine, but not unsupervised. And there will be rules."

"Is he charming? What does he look like?" Eden closed the dishwasher door and returned to the living room. She knelt on the floor by Phoebe, who clapped her hands with glee. Gabby said a silent prayer of thanks she'd been blessed to have Eden caring for the baby while she worked. The woman was a gift from the good Lord.

"I don't know. He's...attractive." She made the word sound as bad as an infectious skin disease. Attractive wasn't a good trait on this guy. "The way Stella was flirting, you'd think she'd have accepted a marriage proposal from him on the spot."

"Stella flirts with every guy under forty."

"True." Gabby hustled down the hall, stowed a laundry basket in her bedroom and loped back. "Here, I can take her."

"Why don't you change quick?" Eden said. "You'll feel better in your jeans."

"You don't mind?"

"Why would I mind? You know I could eat this little dumpling up." Eden scrunched her nose at Phoebe and tickled her tummy. Throaty baby laughter filled the air.

"Okay, I'll be right back." She raced to her room and donned her best jeans and a blouse patterned in various shades of red. With a quick brush of her hair and a swipe of tinted lip gloss, she was ready to face whatever came her way. She returned to the living room, and Eden handed her the baby. The air filled with her little gurgles.

"I can tell you're worried about this situation," Eden said. "But there's no reason to get worked up. He's not the father. And you *are* her legal guardian. You call the shots."

"You're right." She shifted Phoebe to her hip. "I guess I've been scared for a long time, always worrying Sam would show up one day and take her from me." She considered herself a rational person. She wasn't gullible—not anymore, anyway—and she tried to do the right thing. Why was she so agitated?

*Something about him reminds me of Daddy. Of Carl. And I don't allow men like them in my life anymore.*

"He's not the enemy." Eden frowned. "Unless… Did you get a weird vibe from him? Do you think he might be shady? Dangerous? We should call my dad to come over and supervise. No one would dare mess with you with Dad scowling at him."

"No, he seemed fine." She let out a little chuckle. "I don't need a chaperone. I can take care of myself." And she could. She'd taken care of herself and Allison all through their teen years and beyond. And now it was her privilege to take care of Phoebe.

"Well, try not to worry, then." Eden hugged her. "You're the most welcoming person I know. You'll get off on the right foot with him for Phoebe's sake. I know you."

"Thanks, Eden."

"If you're sure you don't want me around, I guess I'll take off. Call me the instant he leaves."

"I will." She held Phoebe tightly. "Thanks again."

After seeing Eden to the door, she took the baby to the couch and selected a children's book from the basket below the end table. For now, she'd try to keep things as normal as possible. And that meant concentrating on Phoebe and not worrying about Dylan.

He'd meet the baby and leave.

Life wouldn't change.

If she kept telling herself that, maybe it wouldn't.

Hopefully, this uncle would breeze out of their lives as suddenly as he'd breezed in.

She'd just have to keep a level head until he did.

# Chapter Two

In and out. Nice and easy. Dylan stared at the 3B on the door inside the apartment building. All he had to do was observe Gabrielle interacting with his niece for a while. He'd know the baby was in good hands, and his gut was telling him Gabrielle wasn't like his mother or his ex. For his niece's sake, he hoped she wasn't. Worst-case scenario? He'd stay in Rendezvous through the weekend to make sure.

After two sharp knocks the door opened, and he straightened, raising himself up to full height. The woman before him had shed her no-nonsense manager outfit to wear formfitting jeans and a colorful shirt, revealing toned arms. She looked younger, less closed off than she had at the inn. Her hair still fell loose around her shoulders. He wanted to touch it.

*Touch her hair?* If he'd been worried about chemistry before, he needed to up his composure tenfold.

At the sight of the baby on her hip, his heart hiccupped. Seeing the child in the flesh was a precious gift—a piece of Sam lived in the bouncing baby girl. With dark curls grazing her neck, rosy cheeks and huge dark blue eyes, she looked as healthy and happy as a child could be. She stuck out her tongue and blew bubbles at him.

"Come in. I hope you found my place okay." Gabrielle held the door open, and he took off his hat as he entered. The apartment itself was beige, on the small side and could use some TLC. The red living room furniture added color to the mix, and the dining table held a vase full of daisies. It was welcoming, he'd give her that. She led him to the living room. "Have a seat."

He lowered his frame onto the couch, not sure what to do.

"This is Phoebe Ann Stover." She smiled at the child with so much tenderness, he almost looked away. He'd never been the recipient of that level of affection. What would it be like to have someone adore him? "She's nine months old, sleeps through the night, loves sweet potatoes and scrambled eggs, but then again, she'll eat anything I put in front of her. She's a happy baby. Sweet as can be."

Sleeping through the night was good, right? Were babies supposed to eat eggs and sweet potatoes? He knew nothing about children. He peered at Phoebe, who held her arms out to him, opening and closing her chubby hands. He hadn't held a baby before. Gabrielle wouldn't expect him to pick her up, would she?

"Want to hold her?" Gabrielle's expression held no malice, but he could see she had questions she wasn't asking. That made two of them.

"Umm…"

The baby lunged for him, and Gabrielle laughed. "Well, it looks like you don't have a choice."

Before he knew it, the bundle of energy was in his

hands. He held her an arm's length away, then eased her closer until her little bare feet rested on his thighs. Soon she was bouncing, her giggles filling the air. She was strong. Watching her push her little legs up and down with so much gusto made him chuckle. Instinctively, he drew her closer. She pressed her palms against his cheeks, and he pretended to blow out a mouthful of air. She laughed. How could such an itty-bitty thing produce such a hearty sound? Someday he'd have to break it to her he wasn't a great comedian.

Someday? It implied an ongoing relationship, and he hadn't thought that far ahead.

"I think it's safe to say she likes her uncle Dylan." Gabrielle wore a wistful expression. "Do you want something to drink?"

Uncle Dylan. He liked the sound of it.

"No, thanks." He made a silly face, and Phoebe laughed harder. She had Sam's eyes. Everything else must have come from her mother. Had Sam even known he was about to have a baby? If his brother could have seen the little girl, he might have had a reason to say no to drugs.

Dylan handed Phoebe back to Gabrielle. She tucked the child on her lap. The baby squirmed, but Gabrielle kept a firm grip on her, distracting her with a pastel bunny that rattled when shaken.

"Would you mind telling me more about her father?" She licked her lips nervously. "I don't have much to go on at this point. When she's older, she'll want to know about him. All Allison said was she saw him playing guitar with a rock band at a bar in Austin. They both had too much to drink, and a month later, she realized she was pregnant."

He winced. Hearing Sam summed up like that didn't do his brother justice. What could he tell her to give an accurate picture of the funny, sensitive kid he'd known and loved?

"Sam was a great guy. He loved music and practiced guitar constantly. School wasn't his strong suit. He opted not to go to college so he and his band could try to get noticed. He worked hard at it. Moved to Austin after high school and played with anyone who would let him. Music meant a lot to him."

He wasn't going to bring up Sam's drug use. He still struggled to make sense of how his talented brother could have thrown away his life on that junk. If he would have checked on Sam more often, maybe he would have noticed the signs.

"How old was he?" she asked.

"Twenty-one."

"The same age Allison was. Do you have a picture?"

He nodded and took out his phone. He scrolled through until he found one from two Christmases ago. At the sight of Sam's smiling face, his chest tightened uncomfortably. The hardest part of the past year was knowing he couldn't talk to or see his brother. One minute they were celebrating Christmas together, the next he was gone.

"What about your sister?" he asked. "What was she like?"

Her face lit up. "She was special. An absolute sweetheart. She, too, skipped college, and worked at the reception desk of a dental practice here in town. I don't want you to think she went around sleeping with guys all the time. It wasn't her personality at all. She…well, I think she must have felt stifled after high school. The nine-to-five grind and living in a small town got to her. A few of her girlfriends decided to fly down to Texas for a weekend, and that's when she met your brother."

The baby let out a sound he could only describe as the hoot of an owl. He met Gabrielle's eyes. They both started laughing.

"Well, I guess that lightened the moment." She hugged Phoebe and kissed the top of her head. "So, Dylan, I don't mean to be blunt, but what exactly do you want? You came a long way. What are your intentions with Phoebe?"

How to answer? He didn't know. He'd assumed he'd check on his niece, make sure she was being raised with love, do what he could to provide for the girl's future and move on as if he'd never met them. He hadn't even considered being part of her life—in any capacity—until tonight.

Seeing the baby with Sam's eyes altered his view, though. What else did his niece inherit from his brother? His musical talent? His sense of humor? Dylan wanted to find out.

"Gabrielle—"

"Call me Gabby."

"Okay, Gabby." Actually, in her home environment she seemed more like a Gabby than a Gabrielle. He shook his head and shrugged. "I don't know what I want."

"I've raised Phoebe since the second she came home from the hospital. She's like my own child. I'm her legal guardian…"

He inwardly cringed. He hadn't realized she thought he might want to fight for custody or visitation rights or

something. In fact, he hadn't considered how his showing up would affect Gabby at all.

*You've been wrapped up in your own world for too
long.*

"I'm not here to claim any rights—I know nothing
about raising babies." He held up his hands, palms out.
"I just wanted to meet her."

But it wasn't true—not the last part at least. He'd
also wanted to check out her living situation and financially support her.

"Well, you met her."

He scanned the room. Tidy. Neat. Although nothing
like the luxurious home he grew up in or the high-end
condo he owned in Dallas, this apartment felt warm
and inviting. The baby seemed to be in good care. He
could leave with a clear conscience.

But he didn't want to.

"I loved Sam. Miss him. This is his child. I want to
be part of her life." As soon as the words were out of his
mouth, his stomach clenched. It was the first commit-
ment he'd made in a long time. Was he up to being part
of his niece's life? He quickly added, "You know, visit
her at times and send her birthday presents and stuff."

"I see." The muscle in her cheek flexed. "What
you're asking for is fair. But I need to know more about
you. I have to know you'll be a good influence on her."

He frowned. She didn't think he'd be a good influence on his own niece? She'd deduced this from the
short time they'd been together? He wasn't sure what
to think about that. Most people fell all over themselves
sucking up to him and trying to win his favor.

But that was because they knew he was rich.

And Gabby didn't.

What would she do if he told her how much he was worth? Would she manipulate him to get her hands on some of the money? His own mother had done it many times. His ex, Robin, had tried, too.

On the other hand, if she didn't know his background, would she find him worthy of being in Phoebe's life?

Was he worthy? He ran his finger under his collar.

He'd been having an identity crisis for a year. When had he lost his confidence?

*When Dad sold the company without even considering letting me run it.*

"I'm starving. Why don't I order a pizza and we can discuss this further?" Gabby rose, lifting Phoebe high in the air. Her little legs kicked as she laughed.

Pizza sounded good. After a year of gourmet meals, high-end hotels and surface conversations, talking to Gabby sounded even better. Normal, even.

How long had it been since he'd been treated like any other guy?

Not in grade school. Certainly not running around with other rich kids at prep school. College—nope—still hanging out with wealthy peers. The four years he'd worked in upper management at King Energy had ensured his days were spent in board meetings, on the golf course or reviewing the performance of the managers below him.

His old world no longer existed. For once he wanted to be an average Joe. But he'd have to be careful not to let Gabby guess his true background. He wouldn't outright lie to her, but he'd be stingy with details.

The trust fund, the child support could wait. Just until he knew her better. Then he'd tell her the truth.

* * *

Why had she invited him to stay for pizza? Gabby paid the delivery guy and carried the steaming box to the kitchen counter. Her stupid heart had softened when he'd talked about his brother. It hadn't been an act, either. Sam's death had broken something inside him—just as Allison's death had done to her. Her pity had kicked in, and she'd invited him to stay without thinking it through.

What had Eden said earlier? She was the most welcoming person she knew. Gabby scoffed. Not a good trait in this situation. She really had to put a clamp on her invitation-prone mouth.

"Let me help with that." Dylan held out a twenty-dollar bill.

"No, thanks. I've got it." She shook her head. "I was ordering one tonight no matter what."

"Really, I want to—"

"No, you're my guest." She held out her hand. "I'll grab a few plates."

At least he'd offered to pay. But then, Carl had at first, too.

She might as well figure out Dylan's work situation while she had him here. Phoebe was playing with the toys attached to the tray of the jumper seat near the couch, so Gabby pulled out a stack of paper plates and napkins from the cupboard. After grabbing slices of pizza, they returned to the living room. She sat on the couch, and he took a chair. Even several feet away, his presence filled the room. He seemed bigger, stronger— more appealing in general—here in her apartment than he had at the inn. And he'd been something special there.

This wasn't a good turn of events. She'd already

nown she was attracted to him, so encouraging more
teraction with him wasn't smart.

She bit into her slice, oozing with mozzarella and
epperoni. Maybe he wasn't slathering on the charm
ke Carl had, but she knew next to nothing about this
trapping cowboy. He could be buttering her up for his
wn purposes. She needed to find out more about him.

"What do you do for a living, Dylan?"

He finished chewing. "I'm not employed at the mo-
ent."

*Bingo.* Unemployed. She'd pegged him as a no-good
owboy the instant she'd seen him, and she always
rusted her instincts.

"What kind of work did you do in the past?" She
ried not to appear too eager for his answer. What had
e said he'd been doing for the past year? Something
bout this and that. Hardly reassuring. He probably went
rom job to job when he got bored or restless.

"I guess you could say I work for hire."

The cheese stuck in her throat. *Just like Daddy. Just
ike Carl.* They'd both traveled as cowboys for hire. Her
ather also occasionally had taken trucking gigs. Know-
ng Dylan was like the two men who'd let her down put
er in a pickle. She had firm rules about cowboys—
pecifically about not dating them. But how did the
ules apply to a relative of Phoebe?

"Is that what you've been doing since your father
nd Sam died? You mentioned being on the road for
he past year."

"Sort of." He took a sip of soda. "I took time off.
Needed to work through some stuff."

How was he paying his bills if he'd been taking time
ff and traveling? If he was like Daddy, he was probably

skimming money from a girlfriend or two. She liked her other idea better—that he was blowing through a small inheritance. But then, she couldn't assume he'd inherited anything. His mom might still be alive.

"Did your mother take your father's death hard?"

He choked and thumped his chest a few times. "Sorry. No, I doubt she's given him a second thought."

Her mouth dropped open, and she quickly closed it.

"They divorced when I was a toddler. No love lost there."

"Did he remarry? And Sam came into your life through the new wife?"

"Dad never remarried. I'm his only child. Sam came into the picture with Mom's third husband."

So his mother had married Sam's father. Made sense. Didn't answer her question of how Dylan was supporting himself, though.

"It's awfully hard to take so much time off when you have bills to pay." She tried not to sound judgmental. But seriously, if he was taking time off and wandering around, how was he dealing with his responsibilities? Every adult had those.

His eyes sharpened and narrowed, but he didn't say a word.

"How have you been supporting yourself?" She didn't care if it was forward. She needed to know—for Phoebe's sake. For her own. And she'd see right through him if he lied to her. She'd gotten good at sifting fact from fiction.

"I don't need much."

Hmm…he wanted to play the ambiguous answer game, did he? She wasn't born yesterday.

"That's a nice truck you drove to the inn earlier."

"It's a rental." His eyes were unreadable. Warning flags waved in her brain. This back and forth reminded her of Carl, but back then she'd been a naive teenager. She'd wanted to accept every lie he told her. She'd believed the best in him. And she shouldn't have.

Most welcoming person or not, she wasn't putting up with any games Dylan wanted to play. Phoebe was too important. Her niece would not grow up being jerked around by some unreliable guy pretending to be something he wasn't. She should know. Until she was eleven years old, she'd thought her father was the greatest man alive. But cold hard facts had shattered her notions about him.

"Look, I know we just met." She set the plate on the end table and locked eyes with his. "In any other circumstances, it would be insulting for me to ask you what I'm about to ask. But this is my niece, and I can't let her be around someone who isn't reliable. Where are you getting your money to live on?"

He blinked once, twice, three times. Then his expression became unreadable. "My dad left me a little something."

Relief spread through her like rain over a dry prairie. She'd been right. He'd come into some cash. Blowing through a small inheritance she could handle. Preying on gullible, lonely women, she could not.

"And you returned home because the money's running out?" She didn't wait for him to answer. "That's fair."

He opened his mouth but didn't say anything.

"What are you going to do next?" She wiped her hands off on a napkin.

"I'm not sure." His face fell.

There was something broken about him. She knew broken. If it wasn't for the baby, she probably would have fallen apart a long time ago. The brittleness edging her curiosity softened.

"You're struggling with their deaths, aren't you?" she asked.

"Yeah." He nodded, setting his plate aside. "I am. No matter where I go, it doesn't change the fact they're gone."

"The traveling… Have you been trying to escape?"

"Maybe." He drew his eyebrows together. "Looking back… I guess I might have been."

"Does anything help you with the grief?" She'd been blessed with her support group—their prayers and meetings each week had gotten her through the toughest of times.

"Somewhat." Their gazes locked, and the connection between them could not be denied. Flutters filled her chest. "My faith helps me hobble through."

"It gets me through, too. I know I'll see Allison someday."

"I'm glad." He sighed, dropping his elbows to his knees. "Faith wasn't part of my life until a few years ago. As for Dad and Sam… I don't know what they believed." He arched his eyebrows.

Her and her big mouth. "I'm sorry. I didn't think before I spoke."

"It's okay." He seemed to see right through her. "You meant well."

Phoebe started to fuss. She was probably hungry. "I'll be right back. I'm going to fix her a bottle."

A few minutes later, she took Phoebe out of the jumper seat and set her on her lap with the bottle. The baby snuggled in her arms as she drank it. This was one of Gabby's favorite parts of the day. There was nothing more relaxing than having Phoebe cradled in her arms.

"Did you grow up around here?" He had an intent gleam in his eye as he watched them.

"No, Allison and I moved here to take care of our grandma after I graduated from high school. Allison was going into eighth grade." She caressed Phoebe's forehead, trying not to dwell on the other reason they'd moved to Rendezvous. She'd finally seen Carl's true colors. The man she'd dated during her senior year of high school had been living a double life. She'd grown up fast after that.

"What happened to your parents?"

"Oh, they're still alive and well. Mama lives down in Laramie with her boyfriend, and Daddy is probably charming some widow in Montana. I don't talk to them much anymore."

"And it's just you and the baby? No husband?" He didn't seem to be fishing about her love life with an ulterior motive, but what did she know?

"No, just us."

"And you plan on staying here?"

She laughed. "Oh, yeah, Rendezvous is home. I can't imagine living anywhere else. I have good friends here, and I love working at the inn…" She proceeded to tell him about her job and how she loved the town. He asked about the area and before she knew it, an hour had passed.

"I should get going." He stood and took his plate into the kitchen. Then he walked over and touched Phoebe's cheek. "You take care now, little one."

"What's next?" Gabby stood, carrying the baby, and followed him to the door.

"I don't know. Let's sleep on it and talk tomorrow."

"Okay." She frowned. "You can stop by after noon."

He put on his hat, tipped it to her and left. After locking the door behind him, Gabby carried Phoebe back to the couch and stretched out on it. Impressions tangled in her mind.

She wasn't sure what to make of him. He was easy to talk to—too easy. In fact, she'd done all the talking. She pressed her hand against her forehead. What was wrong with her? She was supposed to be finding out if he was worthy of being part of Phoebe's life, not gushing about how much she loved Rendezvous.

Still, he *had* shown his vulnerability when it came to the deaths of his brother and father. But as far as his work history, his future plans…she'd completely flaked out on getting any concrete answers.

And once again she'd invited him over.

In all his travels, he hadn't found this.

Dylan drove across Silver Rocks River and turned onto Centennial Street to drive through downtown Rendezvous. After 7:30 p.m., the sun was still out. Families entered and exited the few restaurants along the street, and once he passed the main businesses, a line appeared around an ice cream stand—the Dipping Dream. He slowed and pulled into a spot in front of a park. Green grass was dotted with picnic tables where people were barbecuing. The smell of grilled burgers reminded him summer had arrived. Rendezvous made it look slower, more fun than he was used to.

Little girls and boys stood near the playground equipment taking turns lassoing a fence post. He chuckled as one of the boys stuck out his tongue and a girl threw down her rope and began chasing him. They looked like they were having a good time.

From what he'd seen of the town, it appeared to be a place where everyone knew each other. He got out of the truck and enjoyed the warm breeze. A white gazebo was nestled in the park. Mature pines partially hid a ball diamond from his view, and he could just make out what appeared to be seven-year-old girls playing softball. Shouts erupted. Proud grandparents and parents stood up cheering.

An unexpected longing hit his heart. This was what community meant. Ice cream stands, barbecues with friends, peewee ball games—all things he'd missed out on as a kid. He hadn't realized until this moment that he was still missing out on them.

Would Phoebe play softball? Would Gabby be in the stands jumping up to cheer her on?

Of course, Gabby would cheer the girl on. It was obvious she loved the baby. Who wouldn't love the girl with her chubby cheeks and cheerful smile?

Earlier when he'd watched Gabby holding her and giving her the bottle, something had shifted inside him. The maternal picture they presented had kicked up a longing he'd never had before. For a brief moment, he'd wanted a child and a wife of his own who would love a baby the way Gabby did Phoebe.

"Na na na na na!" Up ahead, two little girls taunted a group of boys. Another round of chasing ensued. He shook his head. Kids being kids.

Gabby had been easy to talk to. The one red flag he'd had about her was when she'd probed into his financial situation. Why did she want to know what he'd been doing and how he'd been supporting himself for the past year? And what had the comment about his nice truck meant? Had she been trying to figure out how much money he had?

"Charlie!" A brunette in her early twenties waved to a couple of guys strolling toward the metal bleachers.

"Hey, Misty," one said without breaking stride. "You watching the game? Emma's playing."

"I was on my way to get a sundae, but I might as well join you." She jogged over to them, and they all laughed about something. Their camaraderie deepened the stirring he'd been feeling for the past few hours.

Man, he was tired of being alone. He turned in the direction of Dipping Dream.

As he'd listened to Gabby talk about her life and friends here in Rendezvous, he'd found himself wishing she'd keep talking for hours. She seemed so genuine. And when she'd asked, "What next?" he'd had no idea how to respond.

What was next?

He supposed he should return to Dallas to set up the trust fund and child support. It had been a year since he'd checked in with any of his old friends. They'd been growing apart for a long time, though. The only people he'd had contact with at all this year were his lawyer and his financial advisor.

The thought of checking out of Mountain View Inn tomorrow and putting his life back together in Texas weighed on him. He didn't know how to put it together. It all seemed meaningless without…

Maybe it was time to face facts. He'd spent his entire life trying to impress his father and get his attention. Now that Dad was gone, there wasn't anyone to impress.

Dylan slowed as he neared the ice cream stand. He had to figure out what to do with his life. No more traveling around the world, delaying the inevitable.

What would it hurt to spend the rest of the weekend here? He could get to know Phoebe better and find out more information about how Gabby planned on raising her.

Come to think of it, he didn't know much about either of them. He'd gotten so mesmerized listening to Gabby talk about the town, he'd barely asked any questions at all. He didn't know her ideas on school and extracurricular activities. Who babysat his niece while she worked? What church did Gabby attend? Would she spoil the baby or be strict? Did she plan on having fun birthday parties for the girl? How would they celebrate Christmas? Would he be invited?

As he fell into the back of the line, relief mingled with peace.

Yes, he'd stay a few days and gather more info. He'd find out how Gabby intended to raise Phoebe. And if he didn't like what she said, he might have to speak up. In fact, he might have to be more involved with the baby than he originally intended. Money was a poor substitute for a flesh and blood person who cared. He should know.

His niece deserved an uncle she could depend on.

But what if he let her down the way he had his father and Sam?

He firmed his shoulders as Phoebe's smiling face

played in his mind. He'd have to be someone she could depend on.

He couldn't live with himself if he let her down, too.

# Chapter Three

She had to set some ground rules with Dylan. Gabby spooned a bite of mashed carrots into Phoebe's mouth the next day. Half of it dribbled out, and she scooped the orange mush back in. Phoebe clapped her hands, her little mouth working through the bite. Her bib had *She's the Boss* embroidered on it, and the tray of the high chair was smeared with bits of bananas and carrots.

"That's right, peanut, you're the boss, and your uncle better not think he can come and go as he pleases." She scraped the side of the container and fed Phoebe another bite. "You're worth more than that. I know how hard it is to resist a handsome man like Dylan when he breezes into town with a slippery smile and words full of sugar. And I know how much your heart breaks waiting for him to show up on your birthday or to the school play he promised to attend. Don't worry. I will not let him string you along."

She was ridiculously glad she'd told Dylan not to come over until after noon. Saturdays were her one day to be lazy. She'd been relaxing in her pajamas and enjoying every second of cuddly bliss with the baby until she'd finally forced herself to shower and get dressed.

Her clock said it was ten minutes after twelve. Would he stop by? Maybe he'd left town already. *Yeah, right.* Wishful thinking would get her nowhere.

The problem was she'd enjoyed his company a little too much last night.

He seemed less shady than she'd originally pegged him for. But that wasn't saying much. It wasn't as if he'd been in a hurry to cough up answers to the questions she'd presented. The moments when he'd been transparent about struggling with the deaths of Sam and his father had been endearing. But the other moments—the ones where he'd hemmed and hawed about his job and what he'd been doing—had not.

Still, he'd been sweet with Phoebe. Gabby doubted he'd been around many babies, and he hadn't hidden the fact he liked his niece. Then again, Phoebe was adorable—everyone liked her.

The little pumpkin smacked her hands on the tray, her mouth open for another bite.

"Well, excuse me." Gabby gave her another spoonful. "You're hungry today, aren't you?"

A knock on the door caught her attention, and her heart immediately started pounding. It was him. She was sure of it. Number one on her list—find out Dylan's intentions. Number two—set some rules. She'd spell out her expectations for him if he wanted to spend time with Phoebe.

She scrunched her nose at the girl. "I'll be right back."

The high chair was a matter of steps from the door, and she quickly checked the peephole. Dylan. Her pulse went into overdrive. She unlocked the door and let him inside.

"I would have called..." His outfit mimicked yesterday's except he'd swapped out his black T-shirt for a gray one.

"It's fine. Come in." She hustled back to Phoebe and gestured to a dining chair. "Have a seat. We're just finishing up."

He settled into the chair opposite her and glanced around her apartment. Then he tapped his fingers on the table, appearing every bit as uncomfortable as she felt. They hadn't been ill at ease last night. What had changed?

"Did you sleep well?" Gabby finally asked. His name had been on the reservation list at the inn yesterday, but at the time she hadn't realized he was Phoebe's uncle. The reservation had been for one night only.

"I did." He nodded. "My room was quiet and comfortable. The staff was welcoming, too."

She could only assume he meant Stella when he referred to the staff. A flare of jealousy sprang up, but she squashed it.

"I'm glad to hear it." As soon as Phoebe finished the final bite of carrots, Gabby wet a washcloth and began to wipe her face and hands with it. After a bit of fussing, the child was clean. She lifted her out of the high chair and set her on her lap. The previous silence snowballed into awkwardness. She wasn't sure what to say, what to do.

*Get it over with. Find out his intentions and set the rules.*

"So last night we didn't really get around to discussing how to move forward in this new…ah…territory we've found ourselves in." She watched him carefully.

"No, we didn't." He shifted in his seat.

"I want to make sure we're on the same page. Phoebe's needs come first."

"Yes, of course." He sat up straighter.

"I hope I don't come off sounding like a taskmaster, but we need to set some ground rules. You mentioned wanting to be in her life. What specifically did you have in mind? Do you plan on visiting her often? Or would it be easier if you sent her gifts for her birthday and Christmas?"

As he exhaled, his eyebrows drew together. "Umm…"

"And, in the future, I'm really not okay with you showing up unannounced. I'd appreciate having at least a week's notice if you're coming into town."

"Uh-huh." He bit the inside of his cheek, giving him an adorably lost look she hadn't thought possible on such a strapping man.

"It might be tempting for you to try to be the cool uncle, but please don't overdo it. It can be difficult for a little girl without any father figure in her life. I don't want her to get unrealistic expectations about you." Her words came out faster as she brought up each new point.

"I take it that means you're not dating anyone."

"You are correct." Was he fishing? It didn't matter. "Since I'm on a budget, I think it would be inappropriate for you to buy expensive gifts for her, not that you were going to, but it's worth mentioning."

He seemed to consider her words. "What do you have against expensive gifts?"

*Everything if there aren't any feelings behind them.* Her mind flashed back to the necklace Carl had given her before they'd split up. The old ache in her heart flared hot and painful.

She held Phoebe tightly as the girl waved to Dylan and began babbling loudly. His grin was instant, and Gabby's ache was replaced by something new and uncomfortable.

"Children need love. It's easy for them to confuse an expensive gift with emotional closeness." She should know. It wasn't only Carl who'd duped her. Her own father hadn't cared that she and her sister lived in a run-down double-wide trailer and never had enough food. But he always brought a new doll or game after being on the road. New toys didn't keep them warm during long winters. "I don't want her to believe you're something you're not."

"Something I'm not? What do you mean?" His blank stare caught her off guard. Maybe she should have thought this through more before speaking. Sure, men had let her down time and again, but he didn't need to know all that.

She wasn't going to tell him how hurt she'd been by her dad and Carl. She didn't talk about them to anyone.

"She doesn't have a daddy, and if you show up once or twice a year with the latest toy and make a big deal over her, it will be pretty tough for her the rest of the time when you're not around."

"I guess it makes sense." He rubbed his chin. She detected nothing but sincerity from him. "You know better than I do."

"Ba-ba!" Phoebe pointed at him.

He looked at Gabby. "What does ba-ba mean?"

"She calls everything ba-ba at this point."

He made a silly face at Phoebe, who slapped her tiny

palms on the table in excitement. Staring at his handsome features, Gabby was tempted to touch the slight cleft in his chin.

Really, she should not be thinking about the cleft or about touching him!

"How do you plan on raising her?" He turned his attention to Gabby and watched her intently.

What was he getting at? Was he concerned she was doing a bad job? Sure, she often worried she wasn't enough for Phoebe. Shouldn't the girl have a mommy *and* a daddy? And sometimes she felt guilty about working all day, but she loved her job, and Eden was a wonderful babysitter.

"She's in good hands."

"I know. I'm not worried about her physical care." He leaned back. "But as she gets older, how do you plan on disciplining her? How important is her education to you? Are you going to sign her up for sports? Will you screen her friends?"

Gabby was speechless. For Mr. Vague-About-Himself, he'd certainly gotten quite detailed about Phoebe's life. Did he think Gabby wasn't up to the task?

Honestly, she hadn't really considered everything he mentioned. She'd been so busy getting through each day trying to move on from Allison's death, that she hadn't given a ton of thought to Phoebe's future. Maybe she should have.

The creases in his forehead clued her in he might be worried based on his own experience. He'd mentioned his parents' divorce. What had happened in his childhood to make him worry about Phoebe's?

"I'll do my best." She attempted to smile. "I haven't

thought that far ahead. I take parenting day by day at this point."

The unsettling sensation in her stomach made her want to wrap up this visit as soon as possible.

"Are you leaving this afternoon or waiting until tomorrow?" she asked.

"Yeah, about that…" He turned to Phoebe and continued the goofy faces. "I think I'll stay in Rendezvous for a while."

Her mind froze. She could hear her heartbeat. He was *staying* here longer? Was it because she didn't have a ten-year plan for Phoebe?

"A while? Could you be more specific?" Her voice was squeakier than a mouse's. "How long?"

"It's hard to say." He lifted one shoulder, and his mouth curved into a grin.

"Why?"

His warm brown eyes held something she hadn't detected in them until now. Hope.

"I'd like to get to know my niece better."

It was as if a ticking bomb began to count down in her brain. A bomb to disaster.

This was how it started—the charming smile, the proclamation he was staying for a while, the wriggling into her life, the playing with her emotions.

The inside of her mouth turned to sludge as she remembered the months she'd spent hanging on Carl's every word, dropping everything when he called and hushing the voice in her head whispering he was playing her. Carl wasn't the great guy he'd pretended to be. She'd been a fool.

Not this time.

"Look, it's sweet of you to take an interest in Phoebe,

but from what you've told me, I really don't know enough about you to encourage you to stick around."

"What do you mean?" His expression darkened.

"I have no idea what you do for work. You mentioned living in Texas. Do you still live there? And what exactly have you been doing for the past year? Don't say this and that—it's not a real answer."

His mouth dropped open, but she didn't give him time to speak.

"How do I know you aren't a deadbeat?"

A deadbeat?

This was a new one. Dylan almost laughed out loud, but the worry and sincerity in Gabby's stormy gray eyes held him in check.

Here he'd been worrying she'd asked about his finances yesterday in order to gain something, and in reality, she'd been worried he was a deadbeat. A sobering thought.

"I'm not a deadbeat."

"That's what they all say," she muttered, diverting her attention to Phoebe.

"They? Who?"

"Cowboys." She met his gaze again, and he was struck by the fierceness in them.

She thought he was a cowboy? Maybe his boots and hat made him look like one. Outside of the office, jeans and cowboy boots had always been his style.

The funny thing? As a kid, he'd always wanted to be a cowboy. His friend had grown up on a ranch, and Dylan remembered one summer—he must have been thirteen or fourteen—he'd gone over there often to watch the men working cattle. Cowboys were tough and cool and everything he'd wanted to be. His friend, along with the ranch hands, had kindly taught him how to ride and rope.

Yeah, he would gladly be mistaken for a cowboy any day.

But Gabby said it like it was a bad thing.

"Cowboys aren't deadbeats." He crossed his arms over his chest. "They're strong and dedicated, and they never quit. They'd give their lives for the animals depending on them."

He, on the other hand, was not strong or dedicated, and he had quit more than one thing in his life. Gabby didn't need to know all that, though.

"Yeah, well, I wish they'd think about the people who depend on them, too." Someone must have let her down. She reached over and grabbed a pale blue stuffed dog from the counter and handed it to Phoebe, who gripped it with both fists and pounded it against the tabletop while blowing raspberries. "You didn't answer my question. How long are you planning to stay?"

His mind blanked. How could he possibly answer her when he didn't know? If he said a month, would it be long enough? Or too long? What if he liked it here and wanted to stay through the summer?

"A month. At least." His palms grew clammy as he realized he'd committed to being here for four whole weeks, the longest he'd stayed in one spot for over a year. Every ten days, without fail, he'd get restless, pack up and move on. Was he even capable of staying in one spot for a month anymore?

"Well, where are you going to stay?" She sounded as incredulous as he felt.

"I'm not sure."

"The inn isn't set up for long-term guests. It would be expensive."

His lips twitched in amusement. She didn't want him at the inn, that was for sure. In his experience, any hotel was set up for long-term guests for the right price. But she didn't know his pockets were deep. And if he told her the truth, he wouldn't be a cowboy in her eyes anymore.

"I'll find something." He'd have no problem finding lodging for a month.

"Okay, but what are you going to do while you're here? You can't be hanging around my place all the time. People will talk, and I won't be gossiped about."

"I won't give them anything to gossip about." She brought up an interesting point, though. What was he going to do all day while he was here? He hadn't thought this through. He'd gotten caught up in small-town wishes last night.

The stuffed dog hit him in the face.

He blinked, and Phoebe let out a deep laugh, and it grew and grew until the child was practically hysterical. He couldn't help it; he laughed, too.

"Oh, you think that's pretty funny, Phoebe, hitting your uncle in the face." He pointed to her, keeping a teasing quality to his tone so she wouldn't be scared. He picked up the stuffed dog and pretended to make it dance.

After a while her laughter finally settled down, and, grunting, she pointed to him.

"Do you want the doggy?" he asked.

She bounced on Gabby's lap and clapped her hands. He held it out to her, and she snatched it from him and chewed on its ear.

"Didn't anyone tell you not to eat dogs?" He shook his head as she slobbered all over the poor animal's ear. "I can see I'm needed here."

Gabby's tender smile hit him in the gut.

Maybe he'd better tell her the truth. He was neither a cowboy nor a deadbeat. He was just a lost guy living off his dad's money.

She let out a long sigh. "If you're serious about staying, then I have some rules."

She seemed to be big on rules.

"Supervised visits only with the baby." She lowered her chin and gave him a stern stare.

"I wouldn't know what to do with an unsupervised visit anyway."

"Okay, good." She raised her chin level again. "You can stop by for a little bit after supper on weekdays. Not every weekday, mind you, but once you get settled, we can work out a schedule for once or twice a week. Saturdays are my day to relax, so please don't come over then."

So far, the schedule sounded limiting. An hour or two once or twice a week? Would it be enough?

"What about Sundays?" he asked.

"Phoebe and I go to church." Her shoulders relaxed, and the sideways glance she shot him hinted she wasn't as sure of herself as she was coming across. "You're welcome to come with us."

"I'd like that." And he would. He missed regularly attending a place of worship.

"Good, and one more thing. You need to get a job."

A job? What kind of job? A tornado built in his chest as all the possibilities ricocheted off him. He hadn't had a job in over a year, and he doubted Rendezvous had any need for upper management.

"I'm not sure where to look." Was he even qualified for anything Rendezvous offered?

She averted her eyes. "Talk to Stu Miller. One of his ranch hands quit and moved away last year after getting married, and his right-hand man died a little over a month ago. He could use a cowboy for hire. Tell him I sent you."

Instantly, the storm inside him calmed. He didn't have to sift through the possibilities. A position was there for the taking—he could literally *be* the cowboy she thought he was.

But his conscience nagged him. From all visible signs, Gabby lived on a budget, and raising a baby couldn't be cheap. He should set up the trust fund and the monthly child support payments. Relieve some of the financial burden of being a single mom.

But if he did… She might flip from being skeptical to having stars in her eyes. Staying in town for a month with a woman who might try to leverage the baby for his money would leave him too vulnerable.

No, he'd do it his way this time.

And that meant taking a shot at the cowboy life he'd always dreamed about.

"Okay." He nodded firmly. His heart felt light—lighter than it had in a long time. "I'll talk to the guy about getting a job."

She visibly relaxed.

"But you've got to do something for me, too."

"What?"

"Let me spend more than a few minutes once or

twice a week with Phoebe. And I need to know more about how you plan on raising her."

Oh, chicken and biscuits, the man was staying!

This was a disaster. Why hadn't she been firmer when he'd thrown out he was sticking around for a while? This guy could be as slippery as the stones in Silver Rocks River. And, worse, instead of discouraging him from staying by telling him he had to get a job, she'd gone ahead and handed him one.

What had she been thinking?

Stu *did* need help. Badly. But it didn't mean Dylan had to trot over there and work for the man.

What if Dylan liked it here so much he stayed? For good?

She wasn't one to hyperventilate, but her breathing got distinctively shallow. *Stop being dramatic.* "I don't mind discussing Phoebe's care, but I'm the one raising her so I call the shots."

"I respect that." A sparkle in his eyes appeared that hadn't been there previously. It made him even more attractive. "The baby—she's got my brother's eyes, and I couldn't live with myself if I didn't make sure she grew up with anything less than she deserves."

Less than she deserves? Gabby tried not to bristle. What did he mean by that? He talked as if he had something to offer. She thought back to the expensive rental truck and his admittance he'd gotten a small inheritance. Maybe the money had gone to his head.

"I'll see to it she has everything she needs," she said. Phoebe threw the stuffed toy on the floor, and Gabby bent to pick it up.

He crossed his arms over his chest. "And I'll be here if you need me."

Need him? She almost laughed, but he'd said it with a straight face. She hated to break it to him, but she would never need him. Maybe he'd gotten a false impression from her.

"Look, we hardly know each other," Gabby said. "And no offense, but I've got this. I took care of the baby fine up until now, and I'll continue to do so whether you stay in Rendezvous or not. If you want me to take you seriously, I suggest you talk to Stu and get settled. Leave raising Phoebe to me."

The muscle in his cheek jumped. Good. She'd struck a nerve. Just because he'd decided to live here for a while didn't mean he'd stick around forever. If he wanted to be in Phoebe's life, he had to earn the right. And that meant not only getting a job, but keeping it for as long as he stayed. Abiding by her rules. And not expecting her to bend over backward to make him comfortable.

He wanted to be in Phoebe's life? Well, he'd have to earn her respect.

Gabby had no time for anything less. And her niece deserved the best he had to offer. Come to think of it, they both did. And if Dylan couldn't or wouldn't give Phoebe the attention and devotion she was worthy of, Gabby would send him packing with no regrets.

"No one is questioning your parenting skills," he said. "You said it was tough on a girl not having a father figure in her life. I get that. I'm not asking to be her dad or the fun uncle or whatever you think. I want her to have a good life. The same as you do."

Well, she hadn't been expecting those words to come

out of his mouth. A blast of shame heated her neck. Dylan Kingsley was saying all the right things. And she couldn't help thinking he was sincere. Maybe she should put aside her misgivings and give him the benefit of the doubt.

"Okay." She sighed. "If you're serious about staying here for a month or so, I'll meet you halfway on the schedule. I'm also willing to listen to your thoughts on how to raise her. Beyond that, I make no promises."

His slow grin held appreciation and gratitude. And it upped his appeal to a dangerous level.

"Thanks, Gabby. I won't let her down."

She cocked one eyebrow but didn't say a word. He'd better not let Phoebe down. If he did, she'd make sure he regretted it. Only one question lingered—could she remain immune to the handsome cowboy?

The last one had broken her heart, but she was a long way from the gullible eighteen-year-old she'd been back then. She'd learned how to protect herself. No one could break her like Carl had ever again. Not Dylan, not anyone.

## Chapter Four

He could see himself working here.

Stuart Miller's ranch sprawled against the backdrop of blue skies and mountains. Sunday afternoon, Dylan walked past empty corrals toward a weathered red barn. Cattle grazed on a hill in the distance, and everywhere he looked were signs of summer. Green grass and blue and yellow wildflowers covered the prairie. A gurgling river snaked behind the outbuildings. The light swoosh of breeze kept the heat at bay.

The view, the quiet, the vastness of this place filled him with the sensation of coming home. He hoped he'd make a good enough impression to get hired.

He didn't have any real experience with cattle ranching, no references to share. How did a job interview like this work, anyhow?

A tall, older man with a paunch came out of the barn and strode toward him. He looked exactly the way Dylan pictured a seasoned ranch owner would. He wore a cowboy hat, short-sleeved shirt, jeans, leather chaps and cowboy boots. A thick gray mustache covered his tanned, lined face. His piercing blue eyes took in Dylan as he approached.

He squared his shoulders and held out his hand. "Dylan Kingsley. Thanks for agreeing to meet me, sir."

Now that they were face-to-face, Dylan noticed the toothpick he chewed. After a lengthy once-over, the man took his hand, pumped it once and hitched his chin.

"Stu Miller. Coulda used ya last week when we were sorting cattle."

He wasn't sure how to respond, but no response seemed necessary since Stu turned on his heel and strode back toward the barn. Should he follow him? Or was that it? Had he failed some secret test?

"Well, are you gonna saddle up or not?" Stu called over his shoulder, waving for him to join him.

He jogged to catch up with Stu. They strode in silence until they entered the barn. His eyes took a minute to adjust to the dim light. The smell of straw and manure brought him right back to spending summer days at his friend's ranch. He savored the memories of a time when life had kind of made sense.

"Tack room's back there." Stu pointed to the wall beyond the empty stalls. "Grab a saddle, and I'll get your mount. Meet me out front when you're ready."

Didn't Stu want to question him about his experience? Get any info about his previous jobs? Find out if he was qualified?

Was he hired and didn't know it?

He selected his equipment from the orderly tack room, hoisted a saddle off one of the racks and brought it all outside. A pair of quarter horses stood near the fence. Stu was already seated on one.

"You'll be riding Jethro today. This here's Diego."

Dylan made quick work of saddling Jethro, gently patting and murmuring to the beautiful mahogany horse. When he prepared to mount, Jethro's ears angled back as if more than ready to get on with the ride. He patted the horse's neck and kept a loose grip on the reins. It had been a few years since he'd ridden, but it felt natural to be back in the saddle.

Stu gave him a long stare. "Where's your rope?"

He'd forgotten the rope. Of all the dumb moves… A real cowboy would never make such a rookie mistake.

"I'll be right back." Dylan dismounted, secured Jethro's reins to the nearby fence and loped back to the barn to grab a rope. Within minutes he was back on the horse and ready to ride.

Stu urged Diego forward. Dylan rode alongside him. They fell into an easy rhythm. Jethro seemed like a disciplined, smart horse.

"I've split the herd—about 250 head of Black Angus and Hereford cattle—into groups for better grazing rotation. We'll check on the north pasture. Where'd you say you were from?"

"Texas. Dallas area."

"Humph." Stu crossed a bridge over a narrow section of the river and continued on a trail through the prairie grass.

He waited for more questions, but Stu didn't ask any. In fact, he remained silent as they traveled over a ridge, passing a field of tall grass and a small grouping of trees before edging along a creek previously hidden from view. Dylan followed Stu until they climbed another hill, and the rolling pasture spread out before them. Cows—black, brown or tan—and their calves contentedly munched away at the grasses. He and Stu rode along the fence until they reached a gate.

"There's a pond beyond the crest. Let's go have a look-see." They went through the gate and checked cattle as they made their way to the crest. Stu grew more chatty as they neared the herd. "Had to give the 95 blue tag calf a dose of penicillin yesterday. Doing fine this morning. I lost one calf late April. Hate to lose 'em."

Dylan wasn't sure how to respond. His experience as a teen had been limited to riding the horses and learning how to rope. He and his friend hadn't joined the cowboys in working with actual cattle.

"See anything out of the ordinary?" Stu flicked a glance his way.

He straightened in his saddle, looking out over the herd and prairie. What would be out of the ordinary? He had no idea what was normal and what wasn't. All he saw were cattle grazing.

"Looks peaceful to me." He hoped he wasn't missing something obvious.

"Let's get to the pond, then."

Within minutes they'd picked their way over the rockier terrain to the water's edge. Some of the cattle were lying near it. A few were drinking. All seemed calm.

Stu skirted the herd and rode toward a stand of trees. "You see that?"

Dylan peered toward the woods. He saw a black lump moving. "Yeah. Is it a calf?"

"Yep." He signaled Diego in that direction. When they reached the trees, Stu motioned Dylan forward. "Get in there and direct him back. I'll get him back to his mama once you've turned him."

Dylan's palms grew clammy, but he nodded. How was he supposed to direct him back? What if the calf got hurt or ran in a different direction? He didn't know what to do. *God, I don't have any idea how to get this calf out of here. Will You help me?*

Why would God listen to an imposter like him? He had no business being here.

Maybe he should tell Stu the truth—he had no idea how to make a calf behave. But Stu had already taken off. And the calf was moving deeper into the trees. Dylan couldn't stand the thought of the little guy getting hurt. There was nothing to do but guide Jethro into the woods slowly, carefully. The calf wasn't more than fifteen feet away, and the horse seemed to have homed in on the little guy.

Dylan almost signaled Jethro to get right up on the calf, but the horse clearly had experience with cattle. Jethro seemed to be tracking its movements. Dylan began murmuring to the horse, and to his relief, the closer they got to the calf, the more it appeared whatever the horse was doing was working. The calf slowed.

He tightened the reins, and Jethro shook his head, then stopped. The calf stopped, too.

Now what?

Jethro's ears pricked, and Dylan took it as sign. "Go on."

The horse moved around the calf, causing it to turn. Good. Now he just had to get it out of the woods. He urged Jethro forward, and as soon as he did, the calf took off running in the direction where Stu waited. At the last minute, though, the calf changed direction. Stu snapped into action, cut it off and herded the calf back to the prairie with the rest of the cattle.

Dylan was sweating. Had he messed up? It had all been going smoothly until the calf got a mind of its own. Maybe he should have taken a different approach. Then the calf would have gone straight to Stu.

"I'm glad to see you kept your trigger finger under wraps in there," Stu said. "Last thing I need is a lassoed calf being injured as he's dragged over branches and stumps." He stopped Diego and took out a handkerchief from his pocket, wiping his forehead. "Jethro's a good cutter. He knows what to do around cattle."

"I can tell he's smart."

Stu nodded. "We'll check fence on the way back."

A while later they rode back to the stables, took care of the horses and then sat in wrought-iron chairs under the barn's awning. Dylan's nerves began to ping-pong. Stu hadn't asked him any questions about his background or experience beyond wanting to know where he came from.

Would this be the interview? He couldn't lie about his experience, but it would be a shame if Stu sent him packing. After spending a few hours out here, he wanted to spend more.

"We're moving cattle again on Monday." Stu's legs were splayed as he watched Dylan's response. The toothpick between his teeth was still working.

He nodded.

"You can get settled in one of the cabins before then."

He tried not to show his surprise. Did this mean he was hired?

"Payday's every other Friday. You're on your own for meals. You have a horse?"

"Um, no," Dylan said, his hope rising. "I can get one, though."

The toothpick bobbed between Stu's teeth. "You can ride Jethro. He needs to be working. It hasn't been good for him with Josiah gone."

Josiah must have been the man who died. A pang of sympathy hit him. "I appreciate it."

"You know how to operate a tractor?"

"No, sir."

"We'll be baling hay next month. Could use your help with that."

Next month? His conscience dug into his ribs.

"I don't know how long I'll be in town," he said. The split-rail fences around the corrals, the peeling paint of the barn and the worn, if tidy, appearance of the ranch didn't escape him. If he had to guess, he'd say Stu couldn't afford to lose a cent. The man would be better off hiring someone who knew what he was doing. He owed Stu the truth. "I don't have much ranch experience."

"I know." Stu leaned back, eyeing him.

"That obvious, huh?"

"You've got good instincts. You know how to ride and you're strong. You want the job?"

The compliment speared heat through his chest. Stu thought he had good instincts. There was a first time for everything. His father hadn't thought so.

"I do want the job. Are you sure you want to hire me considering I might not stay long?"

"I was born on this ranch. Been at it sixty-seven years. I've seen a lot of restless cowboys. Right now my choice is between you and a couple of fifteen-year-old kids from town. The work's hard. Hours are long. I'll take the help as long as you're willing to stay. But no boozing, no carousing. I've got no use for that on my land."

"You can count on me." He'd gotten the job—he was going to be a real cowboy! Satisfaction filled him as he realized he'd be spending his days in the open air on horseback. Moving cattle—he'd have to figure out how to do that—and checking fence and maybe even driving a tractor to bale hay.

Satisfaction shifted to excitement. "Did you say you have a cabin I can stay in?"

"Sure do." Stu stood. "Come on. I'll take you over there."

They walked past the barn down a dirt lane where he could see weathered wood cabins. Most were tiny. One was larger. And a big log structure was tucked behind them.

"That there used to be the bunkhouse, but about ten years ago, it became more of a meeting place. Two of my ranch hands, Jim and Spud, got married and started families, so they didn't want to bunk together anymore. They live in town. The two-bedroom house was Josiah's before he died. He was my right-hand man for thirty years. His wife died of cancer a few years prior."

Dylan glanced over at Stu. The toothpick moved up and down quickly, and he could see the stress lines around his mouth. It must have been hard on him losing a trusted friend. Then the man pointed to the smaller cabins. "Steer clear of the one on the end. Critters found their way inside. Haven't gotten around to getting rid of 'em yet. This one here's in the best shape. Cade left it clean and tidy before he moved. Got married last month and relocated to Colorado. Why he'd want to live there, I have no idea. Anyway, take your pick."

"The one you mentioned is fine." He wasn't taking the large cabin, not when he'd only be here a month or so. Plus Stu might hire someone long-term, someone with experience who would rightly expect to live there.

The rancher pulled out a full keyring. After finding the correct one, he led the way up the path to the small, covered wooden porch and unlocked the cabin door.

Dylan entered and frowned. His bathroom back in Dallas was bigger than this place. A double bed stood in the corner next to a window. To his right, a row of kitchen cabinets lined the back corner. There was a small stove and a refrigerator, too. A table with two wooden chairs separated the kitchen and the living area, which consisted of an old plaid couch, a rocking chair and an ancient television. Rag rugs covered the wooden floor.

"Is there a bathroom?" He hated even asking the question. What if the answer was no?

"Behind the bed." Stu pointed.

He opened the door and was pleased to see a full bathroom complete with a tub and shower combination. All original with hard-water stains, but at least they were there.

"I'll let you get settled. Take tomorrow off. We meet at the barn at five o'clock sharp Monday morning. If you need me, my house was the one you passed driving in. Here's my cell number." Stu told him the number while Dylan entered it into his phone. He then texted him so he'd have his number, too. "Oh, by the way, you'll want to get some chaps and gloves. If you need an advance, let me know. Rendezvous Outfitters has never let me down."

"Thanks." He shook Stu's hand again. "I appreciate you giving me the job."

"Here's your key." And with that, Stu left.

Dylan looked around the cabin. It was tiny. Ancient. The opposite of luxurious.

And it was the best lodging he'd had in over a year because he had a job. A purpose. He was officially a cowboy.

Yeehaw!

Gabby could use some motherly advice and a woman to lean on. Sometimes she resented the fact her mother showed no interest in her life and had moved on with a stranger down in Laramie. At least Gabby had Babs O'Rourke. Her redheaded, seventy-one-year-old boss was the closest thing to a mom she had here in Rendezvous, or anywhere for that matter.

Their weekly Monday afternoon business meeting in Babs's office at the inn was almost wrapped up. Yesterday Gabby had filled her in briefly about Dylan coming to town, which meant as soon as the meeting ended, Babs would have a laundry list of questions for her about him. Her boss had been the town busybody for years and wouldn't give up the title anytime soon. Gabby didn't hold her gossipy ways against her. She had a heart of gold.

"Now that we have business out of the way, tell me more about this mystery uncle. Stella told me he's hotter than a batch of fries fresh out of the deep fryer. Is he tempting you to change your mind about cowboys?" Babs leaned forward over the desk with her fingers splayed, revealing long red nails. Her short hair had been curled, teased and sprayed, and she wore heavy eyeliner, thick mascara and crimson lipstick.

"No." Gabby held herself primly.

"Give him time, sugar. So what's he going to do? Just sit around town counting down the minutes until he can see you and the baby?" She tapped one of her red talons on the desk.

"No, and so we're clear, he's here to see the baby. Not me." She'd been surprised when she'd gotten Dylan's call yesterday afternoon telling her Stu had hired him. She hadn't expected him to talk to Stu so quickly. She'd figured he'd linger around town until he deemed it absolutely necessary to get the job. "Stu Miller hired him."

"Oh, good. That poor man has had tough times lately. Cade getting married and moving out of state was bad enough, but then Josiah dying…well, it's hard to lose your best friend." She made a clicking sound with her tongue and shook her head. "Isn't he down to two ranch hands? I told Jimmy Ball to send over a few of those high school boys, but you know how it is. Jobs, sports and their own chores leave them little time to work for someone else."

"I do know. I hope Dylan will be a help to Stu."

"Why wouldn't he be?" Babs gave her a questioning look. "You don't think too highly of him, do you?"

She sighed. It wasn't fair for her to project her concerns about cowboys onto him. At least not until he proved her correct. "I don't know him. I'm sure Stu will be happy to have an extra set of hands."

"Don't sound so enthusiastic," Babs said almost under her breath. "Okay, so what do you know about him? He's tall, dark and handsome—I got that from Stella. You say he's from Texas, right? And he's been traveling since his daddy and stepbrother died. Sounds like he needs a place to settle. Maybe Rendezvous will feel like home."

"I hope not." An involuntary shudder rippled down her back.

"Gabby." Babs stared at her hard. "You're concerning me. Now tell me the truth. Is this about your grudge against cowboys or is Dylan a risk to the baby? I will not let my little Phoebekins be put in danger, uncle or not."

"I can't imagine he'd be a risk to the baby. He doesn't seem the type." Guilt nibbled at her. "He wants to get to know her and be part of her life."

"See? That's not so bad. An uncle to dote on her is a good thing."

"I guess."

"When will you see him again?"

"I'm not sure. I expect he'll want to get settled at the ranch. He's staying in one of the cabins there."

"You'll have to let me know next time he comes around. I'll just happen to stop by." Babs raised her eyebrows, her green eyes sparkling. "I need to see this hunk for myself."

Gabby was more than ready to steer the conversation in another direction. "Have you thought more about what you told me on Friday? Are you still set on selling the inn?"

She lost some of her sparkle. "I am. I know you aren't keen on it, but I can't help it. I've unloaded the other properties, and this is the final one."

"But it's your livelihood. Your pride and joy."

Her face fell. "It was. I kept going full-steam ahead after Herb died, but now…"

"I wish you'd reconsider." If she could get Babs to

keep the inn, her life wouldn't be so up in the air. "I'll take on more responsibilities—anything."

"You already run the place, Gabby. It's not the money or the work."

"Then what is it?" She hadn't considered there might be a personal reason—a bad reason—for Babs to want to sell the inn. "You're not sick or anything, are you?"

"No, honey." She shook her head. "You don't have to worry about that."

"Then what?"

"I'm ready to retire for good. I might travel or winter down in Florida or… I don't know. I've been feeling it in my bones. I need to be free. And as long as I own this inn, I'm not free."

Gabby wanted to plead with her, tell her she'd run it single-handedly, but she was being selfish. If Babs wanted to retire and be free, Gabby wouldn't be so heartless as to try to stop her. Besides, she probably needed the money from the sale of the inn to do the things she wanted.

Babs sniffed. "I hate to get you worked up, but there's been some interest in it."

"But it's not even on the market yet." Her heart sank. She thought there would be more time—months preferably.

"I know, but I'm partnering with a real estate agent this time instead of selling it on my own, and Dorothy Wendall put the feelers out."

Gabby took a deep breath. Putting out feelers and getting interest might amount to nothing. She shouldn't let herself get all worked up even if Dorothy Wendall was the best real estate agent in town.

"Do you know who's interested in it?" Gabby asked.

Maybe this wouldn't be so bad. A local could be buying it—they'd know how hard she worked and want to keep her.

"Nolan Hummel." Babs made a production out of straightening the papers on her desk.

Nolan Hummel? The arrogant jerk who'd asked her out more than once and hadn't taken being rejected well? He always looked her up and down like he was evaluating a porterhouse steak. Gabby would rather scrub toilets than work for him.

"Why would he want an inn?" Gabby tilted her head. "His family specializes in shipping. Didn't he get promoted to vice president last year?"

"He did, and I don't know why he wants it, hon. I'm just trying to keep you in the loop. I guess we can ask him when he tours the place."

"He's touring it. When?" She scooted to the edge of her seat.

"I'm not sure. He'll be in town this week, and I'd imagine he'd want to schedule a visit soon."

She gagged a little. There was no way he was buying the inn. He didn't even live in Rendezvous. As far as she knew, Nolan resided almost an hour south where Hummel Freight's headquarters were located. He came to Rendezvous only every few months to check in with his vendors.

What if Nolan moved here? She'd have to see him all the time. And possibly work for him. A dull ache formed behind her temples.

"You said *some* interest. Is anyone else, by chance, interested in buying the inn at this point?" At Babs's shake of the head, she sighed.

"When Dorothy Wendall lists it next week, I'm sure

we'll have more prospects. I'm not a big fan of Nolan, either, sugar. He talks to me like I'm ninety-nine years old and as stupid as a skunk crossing a busy highway. But the Hummels can afford the place, and I know they wouldn't run it into the ground. They know business."

Gabby couldn't argue with that. They did know business, and they'd likely be good owners of the inn.

Too bad she couldn't see herself working for their son. Life was too short to spend it working for someone she loathed. If Nolan Hummel was a serious buyer, she'd have to put feelers around town and find out if anyone was hiring.

But how would she find a job she loved as much as this one? And could she afford to work somewhere else? Good-paying jobs were few and far between in this town.

"Would you at least give me some warning when Nolan schedules his tour?"

"Of course. And don't feel like you need to keep the fact I'm selling the place a secret. The entire town knows. I figured spreading the word might flush out a buyer." Babs pushed her chair back and stood. "Am I still babysitting Phoebe tomorrow night?"

"Yes, please." Tomorrow was Tuesday. Gabby was blessed that Babs loved babysitting Phoebe for her while her support group met in one of the inn's conference rooms. "Thanks for being such a wonderful grandma to her."

"Don't you mean Glam-ma?" Babs preened and laughed. "I'm tickled you let me help out."

She stood and rounded the desk, pulling Babs in for a hug. "I don't know what I'd do without you. I don't blame you for wanting to retire and enjoy life. You deserve it."

Babs gave her a squeeze before stepping back. "I enjoy life plenty. I'm just…well…going through some things. Thanks for understanding. It will all turn out all right. Don't you worry."

"I won't." She pasted on a smile. But the worries were already kicking up in the back of her mind. It hit her that if Babs was retiring and traveling, she wouldn't be around for Gabby or Phoebe. There went Glam-ma… and Gabby's mom away from mom. What would she do without Babs?

He'd never been this sore in his life.

Wincing, Dylan eased his body onto a park bench at the entrance of Riverwalk Park in downtown Rendezvous Monday evening. When he'd called Gabby this afternoon, she'd tried to blow him off about seeing Phoebe today, but he'd gotten her to agree to a walk on the river trail after she finished supper.

He didn't know what model car she drove, so every now and then, he looked back to scan the narrow parking lot for a pretty brunette.

Today had been exhausting. Draining. Somewhat embarrassing. And absolutely fantastic. He had a whole new respect for the cowboys he'd always admired. Until today, he'd never ridden a horse for more than a couple of hours, and he couldn't remember a time he'd done any hard, manual labor. His parents had hired people to do the heavy lifting. Now he knew why.

A long soak in a Jacuzzi would do him a world of good. But he'd have to settle for another sweltering night in his cabin instead. The place didn't exactly have the amenities he was accustomed to. The shoebox with no air-conditioning felt like a sauna. Maybe he could pick up a fan here in town.

"Hey there," a woman called. Gabby pushed a stroller toward him. Her hair was pulled back into a bouncy ponytail, and she wore black leggings ending at her calves, a long turquoise T-shirt and running shoes. "Hope you haven't been waiting long."

"I haven't." He stood, trying not to flinch. Every nerve ending twitched. Every muscle spasmed.

"What's wrong?" She stopped the stroller as soon as she reached him.

"Nothing." He couldn't help smiling as Phoebe grabbed both her bare feet and grinned at him. He bent his index finger to wave to her. "Hey there, smiley. You sure are happy today, aren't you?"

The baby replied by sticking her toes in her mouth. He wished he was that flexible. It sure would make ranch work easier.

Straightening, he met Gabby's eyes, and a burst of anticipation chased away all thoughts of sore muscles. With her flushed cheeks, she had a glow about her, one he could almost reach out and touch.

"Thanks for meeting me," he said. "I know you're probably tired from work."

"A girl needs to exercise." She raised her eyebrows as she shrugged, smiling.

Her trim figure made no argument with that. He extended his arm for them to start walking. "Which way?"

"Hang a right. We'll take the scenic route."

"Want me to push the princess?" He hoped she'd agree. There was something about watching Phoebe's cute face that melted away his worries.

"Go for it." She took her hands off the handles, and he began pushing. They fell into a brisk pace. The warm, sunny evening lured people outside. Several couples and families were on the paved trail. Gabby glanced his way. "What did you do today?"

Where to begin? It had been the longest day of his life, but the time had passed by as quickly as a blink of an eye.

"I helped Stu feed the cattle, then we moved part of the herd to a new pasture." He hadn't been good at moving cattle. Hadn't been comfortable being around them at all. The other ranch hands, Jim and Spud, were seasoned pros, and even the high school kids, Cody and Austin, had known what to do more than him. He'd kind of lagged along, doing whatever Stu told him to do. He hoped his boss wasn't disappointed.

"Sounds like a typical day on the ranch."

"Yeah, we fixed part of a fence where a bull broke through." At least he'd redeemed himself with the fence. For years he'd been strength-training and running daily. Digging holes, hauling fence posts and pounding them into the ground had been the easiest part of the day.

"I guess you feel right at home, huh?" She made it sound like a statement, but when he glanced her way, he noted the curiosity in her eyes.

"It's day one." He wanted to feel at home, but his lack of skills worried him. Stu could fire him at any minute. It had been obvious he didn't know what he was doing. "We'll see how it goes. What about you? Was everything smooth at the inn?"

Her eyebrows drew together, but then her lips curved upward. "It was fine. We're booked through the first week of July, so that's good. The town has a big celebration for Independence Day every year. It's a lot of fun, and I'm glad we'll be able to draw tourists to it."

"I'm assuming the summer months are busiest at the inn." He glanced at Phoebe, who stared contentedly at him and gurgled, still holding her feet.

"For the most part. We do get some visitors as well as hunters and fishermen in the fall. And we're usually busy during the holidays. January through March are the slow months."

"I can see that." The trail wound along the top of the riverbank, and the water below flowed over rocks, kicking up sprays of waves. Between the river, the blue sky, a hawk flying overhead and the mountains in the distance, a sensation of awe and belonging came over him.

"Oh no," Gabby said under her breath.

"What?" He looked around. Besides a few couples strolling their way, a man wearing athletic shorts and a tight T-shirt was talking on a cell phone while power-walking toward them.

"Nothing." The word was clipped. She pulled her shoulders back and kept her pace. When the man saw her, his gaze took her in from head to toe, then he ended the call and pocketed his phone.

Dylan sensed Gabby would have gladly spun on her heel and sprinted in the other direction, but she stood her ground as he approached.

"Gabrielle." The way her name rolled off his tongue irritated Dylan. There was something oily about this guy. The man locked eyes with Gabby. "Good to see you."

"Nolan." Her tone was no-nonsense. "I heard you were arriving this week."

"Then you must have heard you'll be seeing a lot more of me."

"Rumor has it." She blinked pleasantly.

He noticed Dylan for the first time.

Gabby turned to him. "Nolan, this is Dylan Kingsley. Dylan, Nolan Hummel."

Dylan held out his hand, and Nolan eyed it for a moment before shaking it. What was his problem? Was he not worth a handshake? It was an odd sensation to be looked down on. He couldn't remember it ever happening before.

"I see you're raising Allison's child." Nolan nodded to the stroller.

At her sister's name, Gabby stiffened. Dylan longed to touch her shoulder and tell her it was okay. But he didn't know why she was bothered. Had Gabby dated this guy? Maybe her sister had. Or they could be related somehow.

"Yes, I am," she said.

"Noble." His smile didn't reach his eyes.

"There's nothing noble about it. I love her." She widened her eyes and gestured to the trail. "Well, I won't keep you. Enjoy your walk."

He cocked his head. "I had cleared my schedule to be at the inn all day tomorrow, but something came up. I'll see you Friday instead."

"Great." Her tone could have chipped ice. "See you then."

Dylan took a long stride to catch up to her. She wasn't volunteering any information. He wanted to ask her about Nolan, but it wasn't his place.

"Do you mind if we stop a minute?" she asked after

walking in silence several yards. "There's a restroom up ahead."

"Sure." A sidewalk cut into the trail, and he followed her to the small building with restrooms. "I'll wait out here with Phoebe."

"Okay."

When Gabby disappeared into the building, he made funny faces at Phoebe. She kicked her feet and let out a squeal. After a few moments, though, she started to fuss, arching her back. Was she uncomfortable? He wasn't sure what to do. As the fussing turned to a cry, he unhooked the straps and lifted her out of the stroller. She grinned at him, clapping her hands.

"You wanted some sunshine, didn't you?" He sat again, letting her bounce her feet on his thighs as he kept a firm grip under her arms. Funny, how natural holding her felt. And it was only his second time. "Do you know what? Your uncle Dylan has never been this tired and sore in his life. I rode Jethro for hours, and my legs feel like jelly. Watching you bouncing your little knees makes my joints ache."

She giggled, and on impulse, he hugged her to him. Who knew such a tiny baby could erase his troubles? She squirmed, so he moved her back to bounce on his legs. She jammed her fist into her mouth, drooling.

"You know what else, smiley?" The entire day came back to him—the exhilaration of working with the men, the embarrassment of not knowing what he was doing— and he realized he needed to share it with someone, even if it was a baby. He used a gentle, singsong voice. "I was a real cowboy today. I helped move cattle from one pasture to the other. Some of those calves and their mamas were slow. Real slow. So we left them alone. Stu told me we'll move them tomorrow. You know what else? I have my own cabin, and it's teeny. As bitty as you are. In fact, I've never slept in something so small. I kind of like it, even if it is hotter than a furnace."

She let out a happy squeal.

"I know, that's how I feel, too. It's good to be alive, isn't it?" He closed his eyes as the words sank in.

It *was* good to be alive. He wished Sam and Dad could still enjoy a perfect summer day.

"Hey, sorry about that." Gabby loped over to them.

"No problem. Is everything all right?" He stood to set Phoebe back in the stroller. He had no idea how to get her strapped back in.

She took Phoebe from him and kissed her cheek, then she lowered her back into the stroller and secured her. "Yeah, Nolan isn't my favorite person. And unfortunately, I can't ignore him. My boss might be selling the inn to him, so I have to be on my best behavior."

"Why?" He tucked away the information.

"Why isn't he my favorite person? Or why do I have to be on my best behavior?"

"Both."

She pushed the stroller to the trail once more. "He thinks he's a big shot, but he'd be nothing without his daddy's money."

The words stabbed his heart. She could have been talking about him.

"Anyway, I'll leave it at that." She fell into a fast pace. "How's your cabin? Do you have everything you need?"

"I'm getting there." But he wasn't. The bedding was threadbare, and he didn't have even the basic items needed to live, like more than a day's worth of food and supplies. "Has that guy bothered you?"

"Yes and no. His attitude bothers me. Other than that, he's harmless." Her footstep faltered, but she adjusted her balance. "Don't worry about Nolan. I certainly won't."

He'd have to take her word for it. But it was obvious she wasn't telling him the whole story. His spirits sank. Why *would* she confide in him? He was merely the uncle she was being forced to deal with.

When they reached the end of the paved portion of the trail, they turned back. Gabby began telling him about how the town raised funds three years ago to pave the river trail, and although he enjoyed her enthusiasm, he listened with half an ear.

She didn't want to tell him about her personal life. He got it. The problem was besides Phoebe—who had no idea what he was talking about—Gabby was the only person he even remotely wanted to tell about his.

Loneliness smacked him square in the middle.

He finally had something worth sharing but no one to share it with.

He was playing at being an uncle, playing at being a cowboy, playing at being part of a small town. Something told him he was going to walk away from Rendezvous disappointed if he played at being important to Gabby.

He wasn't important to anyone. The story of his life.

# Chapter Five

"Everything is going off the rails, and I don't know what to do." Gabby hung her head Tuesday night. She'd told herself again and again to stay positive and not to flip out, but as soon as Nicole, Eden and Mason walked into the conference room for their weekly support group meeting, she'd lost it.

"Hey, what's wrong?" Eden immediately sat beside her, putting her arm around Gabby's shoulders.

She looked from one concerned face to another. Mason was frowning, and Nicole was massaging her very pregnant belly.

"Babs is selling the inn, one of the potential buyers is not my favorite person and I've seen Phoebe's uncle three times in four days. It's a bit much."

"I heard Nolan was in town asking about the inn." Eden's lips puckered like she'd sucked on a lemon. "He isn't considering purchasing the place, is he?"

"He might be." She shouldn't have said what she did. It wasn't fair to Babs or Nolan. Her feelings weren't a factor in the deal.

"Are you worried you'll lose your job?" Mason asked.

"Yes." And she was worried about more than that. "If I don't like the owner, I'm even more worried about keeping it."

"I'm sorry, Gabby," Nicole said. "Stella told me it was going up for sale. Thank you for hiring her. I think having a steady job is grounding her."

Gabby doubted it, but she wouldn't disrespect Nicole. "I'm glad to have her at the front desk. Customers like her cheery smile." If only she could inspire some ambition in Stella to want to actually perform her duties without Gabby nagging her.

"You won't move, will you?" Eden chewed the corner of her bottom lip.

"Move? Of course not! Where would I go?"

"To another town where you can manage another hotel. A nicer one." Eden's face fell. "You're really good at it."

"You'd make more money if you moved to Jackson," Nicole said. "Think of the swanky hotels they have."

"My home is here." Gabby glanced at Eden, who looked unusually emotional. "I'll make it work."

"You mentioned the uncle. How is he? What's his name again?" Mason crossed his leg so his ankle rested on his knee.

"Dylan Kingsley. And he's working for Stu."

"He's a ranch hand?" Mason sounded surprised.

"He's a cowboy." She shouldn't sound so disgusted, but she couldn't help it.

"Here we go…" Mason said under his breath as he averted his eyes. Eden actually rolled hers. Gabby didn't care. They had no idea how much pain Carl had put her through, and she wasn't going to enlighten them now.

"What's wrong with a cowboy?" Nicole's cheeks were flushed.

"Nothing." Gabby raised her hands. "Everything."

"Well, which is it?" Nicole looked confused.

"I don't know. My daddy was a cowboy for hire, and let's just say I thought the world of him until I realized he was cheating on my mom with women all over the state."

"Oh, I'm sorry." Nicole winced.

"Don't be."

"Not all cowboys are cheaters." Nicole's tone soothed the tension.

Maybe not, but the ones she'd trusted had been. "I don't have time in my life for a cheater or a liar."

"Let's change the subject," Eden said.

"Sorry, guys, I'm superstressed." Gabby slumped, overwhelmed by all the changes. "With losing Allison and raising the baby and now a mystery uncle and I might lose my job…"

"I get it, Gabby." Nicole's sad eyes met hers. Shame zipped down her core. Her own problems were miniscule compared to Nicole's. How could she complain when Nicole lost her husband and was pregnant with triplets? "I've been struggling, too. There are too many what-ifs for my taste. What if the babies come early? What if they come late? Will I be able to take care of them all? And then there's Mom…she's dating a new guy…not that it matters. Sorry to hijack the conversation. Is there anything we can do to help you?"

"I'll be fine. I have nothing to complain about." Gabby shook her head. She hated indulging in pity parties. "We'll all help with the babies in any way we can, so try not to stress about them too much. And what's going on with your mom? Don't you like the new boyfriend?"

"He's okay. She's head over heels. As usual." Nicole shifted, wincing. "Why don't we get into our Bible reading?"

"I'm dealing with some stuff, too." Eden's eyes had grown round.

"What is it?" Mason leaned forward. "What's going on?"

"It's nothing like what you're all going through." Eden's face crumpled. "It's just that Mom and Dad are making some changes, and I don't know how I fit into them."

"What kind of changes?" Gabby asked. She couldn't imagine the Pages doing anything other than what they'd always done. They owned a large cattle ranch outside Rendezvous, and Eden had gone away to college for a few years before moving back home to be near her sister, Mia—Mason's late wife—while Mia had cancer treatments. After her death six months later, Eden had stayed at the ranch to babysit Noah for Mason. Eden never mentioned wanting to do anything else.

"They're talking about buying an RV and traveling around the country." Her expression gave Gabby the impression of a lost little girl. "It's bizarre."

"Would you go with them?" Nicole asked.

"No." She shook her head as if it was the last thing she'd ever do. "An RV sounds awful. I want to stay on the ranch. It's my home."

"We'll look after you," Mason said.

"Thanks," Eden said. "I've gotten used to life back home. And now it's going to change. Again."

"Well, one thing isn't going to change. You'll always have us." Gabby reached over and squeezed Eden's hand.

"I want to believe you." Eden sighed. "But it's obvious things are changing for all of us. Mason, you're married now. Nicole, you're having triplets and starting over after years away. And, Gabby, the new uncle and possible job loss don't reassure me you'll be staying in town even if you want to."

"Hey, don't get worked up, it will be all right. I'm not going anywhere." Gabby squeezed Eden's hand.

"Remember what you've been telling me for years?" Mason leaned back in his chair. "God's not going to desert us. He's got this."

"I wish my faith was as strong as yours." Nicole shifted in her seat. "Sometimes I feel like my life keeps going from bad to worse. I wish I could get a job. Then I could afford my own place. It's…hard right now, living with Mom and Stella."

Gabby couldn't imagine living with her mom again after so many years of independence.

"We have a lot to pray about tonight," Gabby said. "Where should we start?"

Mason cleared his throat. "If you don't mind, I'd like to share something I came across when I was reading my Bible this week. I think it fits well with what we're talking about. It's from John 14:27. 'Peace I leave with you, my peace I give unto you: not as the world giveth, give I unto you. Let not your heart be troubled, neither let it be afraid.'"

Gabby let the words sink in. The Lord didn't give as the world did. She wanted His peace. But she didn't know if she could prevent her heart from being troubled, not with her personal anxieties mounting. Thinking about her friends' problems wasn't helping, either. But that's what prayer was for. *Father, I need You. Give me Your peace. Help me lean on You. Help my friends, too.*

Dylan came to mind. It had been pleasant to walk with him last night even though they'd crossed paths with Nolan. In a strange way, she'd been glad Dylan had been by her side. His presence had been a buffer between her and the threat to her job Nolan represented. Afterward, she'd wanted to lean on Dylan, to share her worries about her job. But she hadn't, and it was for the best.

"Okay, where did we leave off last week? Philippians?" Gabby shoved everything out of her mind. Sharing with Dylan, opening up to him, would only lead to trouble. She had enough of that right now. Why ask for more?

"Haven't you ever fished before?" Stu took a step back as Dylan held a fly-fishing rod in one hand and an empty spool in the other.

"Can't say that I have." He had no clue what to do with any of the equipment Stu had brought. An hour ago, they'd finished checking the cattle and taking care of the horses, and Stu had told him they were going fishing—they'd earned it. Since Gabby had some meeting on Tuesday nights, Dylan hadn't objected. But his stomach was roiling as once again he looked like a complete fool.

"Don't they have rivers in Texas?" Stu's ever-present toothpick bobbed as he spoke.

"They do. I've just never been fishing."

"Well, come on then. I'll teach you. A man should know how to fish." Stu dug around in his tackle box and tossed a few plastic containers Dylan's way. "Attach the backing to the rod, then you can attach the line and the leader."

He shuffled the plastic containers until he found one with the backing label on it, then he stared at the reel. How was he supposed to attach this and whatever else Stu mentioned, and why were there so many things involved?

"It snaps off." Stu took the reel out of his hand and lifted one side. "The orange line is the backing. Wrap it around the reel twice, then tie it with an anchor knot. If you move it back and forth a few times, it'll get nice and snug. Then you can attach the line."

Heat rushed up his neck as he tried to process what Stu wanted him to do. What length of backing should he wrap around it? Did he cut it first? And what was an anchor knot?

"Okay, so I gave you a good all-purpose size rod." Stu opened the package and pulled out a few feet of backing. Then he wrapped it around the reel, leaving about three inches dangling. "Here, you can tie the knot now."

Was he sweating bullets? It was bad enough he revealed his ignorance about the ranch on a daily basis—how was he going to explain to Stu he didn't know what an anchor knot was? For the first time in his life, he wished he'd had some wilderness training.

Stu was busy preparing his own rod and reel. He finished attaching everything in what seemed like one minute flat.

"Would you mind demonstrating the anchor knot?" He wanted to crawl under the rocks across the river and never come out. But more than that, he wanted to fish and try everything a ranch in Wyoming offered.

"Didn't your daddy teach you anything, son?" He didn't look mad or even sarcastic. His expression was curious.

Dylan winced. His dad had taught him things—to do his best in school, to not waste time on hobbies, to dominate at football, to network with the right people. Dylan had tried to live up to his standards, but he'd never met his expectations. Even working for Dad's company had been a joke—the man had never seriously considered passing it on to him. He just wished he would have realized it before Dad sold it.

"My father ran his own business and didn't have much time for leisure." The sad truth was, his dad had considered him unworthy to take his place. Why else wouldn't he have had the decency to let him know he'd sold the company? Dad's administrative assistant had told Dylan a solid thirty minutes before the news went public. He could still taste the metallic tang of the emotional sucker punch. His father should have warned him, not misled him into thinking he truly had a shot at running the company someday.

"If you don't have time for leisure, you're not living. Life isn't all work." Stu gestured to the reel. "Hook it over like this…" As Stu demonstrated what to do, Dylan paid close attention to his instructions, and soon his rod was ready for fishing.

"Now you want to get the rod to bend and stop twice. Once behind, once ahead. And you want to keep the tip of your rod straight so you can get your line to follow a nice, straight path. When you bring the rod back, don't

o too far. You don't want your line falling behind you
n the grass."

It took several tries, but eventually Dylan was cast-
ng in a reasonably straight line. He stood on the riverbank and marveled at the clear water running over the
rocky bottom.

"Did your father teach you how to fish, Stu?" He
glanced over as the man cast his line several feet up-
stream.

"Yes, he did. I was a little tyke, and I remember
tagging along with him everywhere. I might as well
have been a burr on his side when I was a young'un.
He taught me everything. How to ride my horse, how
to rope a cow, how to work cattle, how to repair things
around the ranch. Hunting, fishing, you name it, he
taught it to me."

A sudden longing pinched his heart. It would have
been nice to have had a father like that.

"Do you have siblings?" Dylan asked.

"Two sisters. One's over in Cody, and the other's in
Florida. Ma and Pa both passed away."

"My dad died, too. A year ago." The sound of line
whizzing through the air mingled with the water rush-
ing over the river rocks.

"I'm sorry to hear that. Your ma?"

"Still alive. I don't see her much."

Stu stared at him but didn't ask questions. They continued fishing. Dylan tried to picture his own father
showing him how to fish. The idea made him laugh.
Even if Dad had taken him out here, he just would have
pinpointed all the ways Dylan was doing it wrong. The
only things Dylan had gotten right in his eyes were
sports and, well, that was it. His father had been proud

of Dylan's high school football days. As a star receiver his height and athleticism had served him well. He'd even been offered a scholarship to a small university in Arizona, but Dad had scoffed at him getting a degree from there, so he'd passed to attend a more well-known school.

He gripped the rod tightly, casting it again, but the line arched over his head and landed in the water with a plop. Maybe his dad had been right not to consider him to take over the company. If Dylan couldn't even stand up to him about what college he wanted to attend, he doubted he'd have had the steely strength to run the company the way Dad had. Now that he thought about it, King Energy had never quickened his pulse the way ranching with Stu did.

"Get it nice and straight." Stu made a motion with his wrist.

Dylan sighed and forced himself to do it the way he'd been shown. This time the line raced out ahead of him easily. It served no purpose to keep thinking about his late father. Still, he wondered what would Dad think if he could see him today? Fly-fishing. Ranching. Sleeping in a tiny, rustic cabin. Hanging out with his niece and her pretty aunt.

He'd shake his head in disappointment. Manual labor? Not for the Kingsleys. Fishing? A waste of time. And he'd throw in his two cents about being on his guard concerning Gabby. There would be the prenup lecture Dad insisted on giving every time Dylan talked to a woman.

Nothing he did had ever been good enough.

"Hey, you got one!" Stu pointed to where his line disappeared in the water. "Jerk up to set the hook. Don't pull too hard. I'll get the net."

He flicked the rod up and water splashed. Then he reeled in the line, his excitement mounting as the fish on the end battled him.

"You've got it! Keep with him." Stu stood next to him with a large fishing net. "Okay, ready? Raise the rod to get his head above the water, and I'll scoop him in."

Dylan followed his directions, and to his amazement, Stu raised the net high holding a big flopping fish.

"You did it, and on your first try. That there's a beauty, too. Good work." Stu's grin spread from ear to ear, and his toothpick dangled out the side of his mouth as he worked to get the fish unhooked. "Brown trout. See the golden color? The black spots give it away. Hoo-boy, this must be eighteen inches. We're frying him up tonight."

As Dylan listened to Stu explain how they'd fillet the fish and cook it, a surge of appreciation filled him. Stu's dad had taught him what he needed to know, and Stu was passing on the knowledge to him.

"Your father sounded like a good man, Stu."

The rancher paused, his toothpick bobbing, then he nodded. "Every kid should have a father like mine."

The peace of the blue sky and dancing river seeped in, and he began to see his father through a different lens. Dad had never taken the time to teach Dylan life skills or show him how to run the company, but Dylan hadn't asserted himself, either. And he had never been passionate about oil and gas like Dad was. Maybe they'd both been at fault.

It was over. He had to start moving on with his life, not stay stuck in the past.

Dylan helped Stu gather the tackle box and gear. If he ever had a child, he wanted to be the kind of dad Stu's father had been. "Thank you for teaching me today. In fact, thank you for everything."

"Sure thing. Come on, let's go have ourselves a fish fry."

As they headed back, Dylan thought about Phoebe. Who would teach her how to fish? Would Gabby get married? If she did, what kind of man would raise Phoebe? If Gabby didn't marry, would Phoebe learn everything she needed to know?

She should have a good father. One who would teach her things, one who would be there for her. One she could count on.

He wanted to be a man people could count on.

He wasn't there yet, though. When was the last time anyone had been able to count on him? He didn't know, and he didn't care to think about it anymore. His fish was waiting.

She shouldn't have invited him over. The next evening, Gabby, with Phoebe on her hip, escorted Dylan to her kitchen. His hands were full of takeout food from Roscoe's Diner. He set everything on the kitchen counter.

It had been a long day at work. A long, boring day listening to Stella compare and contrast the good points of local cowboys Cash McCoy and Judd Wilson. Honestly, Gabby had strived to be patient at first, but it hadn't taken long before she'd done everything in her power to avoid Stella's mindless chatter. In the end, she'd given up and picked up her phone for a distraction. Dylan was the first person to come to mind. Hence, the invitation for him to come to her place for dinner. The fact he'd immediately offered to pick up burgers from Roscoe's had made it worth it.

"This smells amazing." She peeked into the bags. "Did you order fried pickles, too?"

"And onion rings. I'm starving." He reached beyond her for the plates. His forearm extending in front of her reminded her all too well he was a strong guy. Her stomach flip-flopped. She blamed it on being hungry. Not on him and his muscles.

"Stu taught me how to fly-fish last night." He sounded excited.

"Oh yeah? How'd you do?"

"I caught one. A big one."

"Now you'll be telling this tale until it becomes legendary." She couldn't believe she was teasing him. She'd known him less than a week. Letting down her guard already. Had she learned nothing from her past mistakes?

*Oh, lighten up, already!*

"It was a trout. A brown trout. And it was seventeen and a half inches long." His eyes twinkled.

"Next time you tell it, it will have grown to twenty inches. In ten years, it will be thirty."

"It'll still be seventeen and a half." He unwrapped the burgers and set them on two plates. Phoebe shifted in Gabby's arms and held her arms out to him.

"Looks like she wants you." Gabby was curious to see how he'd respond. The other night on their walk, she'd been surprised to see him holding Phoebe after she finished up in the restroom, especially since he hadn't seemed very comfortable around the baby before.

"Come here." He wiped his hands down his athletic shorts then took Phoebe from her. He lifted her smiling face above his and made silly faces at her. She squealed, kicking her legs. Then he brought her back down, holding her firmly against his side. The picture they presented sent a rush of longing through Gabby's heart. She never let herself play the what-if game, but what if she had a husband, a partner to help raise the baby?

"I'll bring the food over." She took the plates full of burgers and sides to the table. He sat across from her. "Do you want ketchup or ranch dressing to dip?"

"Both. Why not?" He continued with the goofy faces as Gabby left the table to get the condiments. He really was good with the baby. But it didn't change anything. And entertaining her wasn't the same as taking care of her. She returned to the table with ketchup and ranch dressing.

"Here, I'll put her in the high chair so you can eat."

"Thanks." His appreciative smile brought heat to her cheeks. Avoiding touching him, she quickly strapped Phoebe into her high chair and gave her a small handful of puff cereal. Then she sat back down.

"So how is everything going at Stu's? I know he's been shorthanded." She took a bite of the burger. So good.

"It's great. We finished moving cattle, and we've been checking calves, fixing fence and looking over the hayfields. I guess we'll be baling next month. He's hired a couple of teenagers to work for a few hours every morning, so that's helping a lot."

Next month? Was he planning on staying longer than his original month?

"Stu's a nice man," she said. "Keeps to himself, but he's always willing to help when a neighbor's in trouble."

"He's helped me more than he'll ever know." He bit into his burger and turned his attention to Phoebe.

What did that mean? He'd been working for Stu for a week. What could the man have possibly helped him with in such a short amount of time? She munched on an onion ring. Maybe the money. Had Dylan needed a job more than he'd let on?

A pit formed in her gut, and the onion ring suddenly tasted burnt. Was he smoothing the way to make her feel sorry for him so he could ask her for money?

Carl had done it so deftly, she hadn't known what had hit her until she'd found herself loaning him money for his electric bill, his car repairs—whatever emergency cropped up on a regular basis—and always with the assurance he'd pay her back as soon as possible.

She was still waiting. He'd never repaid her one red cent.

"What do you mean? How has he helped you?" She prepared herself for a sob story about his bills.

His face grew red. "My dad wasn't the outdoors type, and Stu has been teaching me things I never knew how to do."

Relief spilled through her as cool as a morning rain, and it was chased by shame. She had to stop thinking the worst about him. "Like what?"

"Well, fishing the other night, for one thing. And how calves like to hide in ditches. The warning signs of foot rot. Why he rotates the herd so often."

"Is his ranch so different from the ones in Texas?" She glanced at Phoebe who had a piece of cereal stuck to the outside of her fist as she attempted to feed herself another piece.

He finished chewing and his forehead creased. "He's different. He's patient."

She couldn't argue with that. Stu was one of a kind.

"Has that guy, Nolan, been back at the inn?"

"Not yet. He's coming Friday for a tour."

"If he buys the place, how will it affect you?" He finished off the burger as he waited for her to answer.

"I'm not sure. Best-case scenario, I can continue my position as day manager. Worst case? He fires me to run it himself."

"What would you do then?"

Her throat felt clogged all of a sudden. She hadn't done any preparation for the worst-case scenario. If she began talking to the locals about job openings, everyone would assume she didn't want to remain on as the manager—and she did. Very much. But if she didn't find out who was hiring, she might be out of work in the event she did lose her job. It felt like a no-win situation.

"I have options." She kept her voice firm, but inside she quaked. Did she have options? And if so, what were they?

"Are you worried about it?"

She nodded, not trusting herself to speak.

"I can help…" His words trickled off as if he wished he wouldn't have spoken up.

"I don't need help."

"I'd like to contribute financially. For Phoebe."

"No, thank you." She should be touched he offered, but she'd seen too much, been through too much, to take him seriously. "Money always complicates things."

He blinked and averted those gorgeous brown eyes. His expression had been sincere, but he'd clearly thought better of the offer as soon as it was out of his mouth. He was probably relieved she wasn't holding him to it.

Phoebe let out a series of loud noises and slapped her

palms on the tray. Gabby was still finishing her final bites, but she moved to get her out of the high chair.

"Let me. Finish eating." He rose, gesturing for her to stay seated. "Is it okay if I get her out and sit her on my lap?"

"You might want to wipe her hands first. There's a box of baby wipes on the counter, or you can wet a washcloth."

He took out a wipe from the container.

"Okay, Phoebe, I see you liked the cereal." He gently wiped her hands, which she tried to keep out of his reach. She grunted in irritation. "But you liked it a little too much, so let's get you cleaned up."

Gabby couldn't get over his patience. He talked in a low, soothing voice as he wiped her hands carefully. Then his face twisted in confusion. "How do I get her out?"

"Press the buttons under the tray." She made a motion with both hands to demonstrate.

"Right." It took him a few moments, but he got the tray off and soon freed Phoebe. As he sat back down with the baby on his lap, Gabby suppressed a longing sigh. She wished Phoebe had a daddy. A real daddy.

But she couldn't let just anyone into her life—their lives. Only the best for her baby niece. Only the best would do.

## Chapter Six

Friday evening as the sun grew hazy on the horizon, Dylan surveyed his cabin and groaned. He had to buy some supplies. New bedding, towels, more food, a coffeemaker—and a fan. Definitely a fan.

In Dallas, he'd spent the hot days in air-conditioning and had relied on restaurants and takeout for meals. Even when traveling he'd never worried about food because he could always order room service. But this week's PB and Js were wearing thin, and all the physical labor was making him hungrier than ever. Earlier he'd driven into town after finishing up his ranch chores to pick up a pizza. He'd called Gabby to see if she wanted to share it, but she'd told him she had plans. He'd wanted to ask what plans and with whom, but he'd ended the call with a *maybe another time* and had been fighting a sense of dejection ever since.

This week had been incredible. His body was adjusting to riding a horse for hours at a time. His palms had grown callused and weren't as tender as they'd been on Monday. Best of all, he'd been able to spend a few evenings with Phoebe and Gabby, and he was starting to feel comfortable with them, too.

But his conscience kept prodding him. Gabby worked hard to provide for herself and the baby. And now she was worried about losing her job. Shouldn't he be getting the child support and trust fund in place for her? Take some of those burdens off her pretty shoulders?

Before he could talk himself out of it, he dialed Edward Brahm, his lawyer. Ed had been his dad's lawyer as well as a close family friend. Dylan trusted him.

"Well, what do you know?" Ed's voice boomed through the line. "You're still alive after all. I thought you'd fallen off the face of the earth."

"You might think I did when you hear where I'm at." He'd always enjoyed bantering with Ed.

"Why? Where'd you land?"

"Wyoming. On a cattle ranch."

"A cattle ranch? Did you buy one or something?"

"No, I'm working on one as a ranch hand. Temporarily."

"A ranch hand?" He guffawed. "Now I've heard everything. You know all you have to do is call Steve if you're having trouble accessing money."

"Haha, funny." Steve Zosar was Dylan's financial advisor, not that he'd ever had trouble accessing his cash. "My money's fine. I'm calling for a different reason. I found out Sam has a child."

"A child? Are you sure about that?"

"Yes, I am." He crossed over to the window where the pastel colors of the sunset spread low in the sky. "I came out here to meet her. Her name's Phoebe. She's nine months old."

"Hmm." Ed took his time before continuing. "That doesn't explain why you're working on a cattle ranch."

"It's complicated, but I'm… Well, I'm happy."

"Good. I know losing Sam and your dad was tough." The teasing was replaced with his business tone. "What can I help you with? I'm assuming this isn't just a friendly call."

"You're right, although, I will admit it's good to hear your voice." Dylan weighed what to say. Maybe he was looking for advice at this point. "I'd like to financially provide for the baby. Set up a trust fund. Monthly child support. That sort of thing."

"Is there something you aren't telling me? You sure this isn't your kid?"

"If it was, I'd have claimed her already." The thought of Phoebe being his own daughter quickened his pulse. It had been a long time since he'd considered being a family man. "How soon could you get something worked out? And what would be involved?"

"It depends. You'll want to spell out precisely what you're providing and the terms of the agreement. Needless to say, your father had his share of women troubles when it came to money, so I suggest extra prudence."

"Yeah, I don't need to be reminded." Gabby's smile came to mind, and her tell-it-like-it-is personality had already convinced him she'd never be like his mom or Robin. But one week wasn't enough to know for sure, was it? He'd thought Robin was perfect until her true colors came out, and that had taken some time.

"First things first," Ed said. "Are you sure the kid is your brother's?"

"She's got his eyes, Ed."

A muffled grunt came through the line. "Do you

have amounts in mind for the child support? And how do you want the trust fund set up?"

They went back and forth on the terms and amounts until Ed had no more questions.

"I'll have my team work on these, and I'll call you when they're ready."

"Don't rush." He hesitated. "I haven't exactly told Gabby who I am or what I'm worth."

"Good. It might be best if she doesn't know at this point. Wait until the papers are drawn up. Then she won't be able to use the knowledge to her advantage."

"She's not like that."

There was a long pause.

"Look, Dylan, I know there are nice girls out there. But until you're sure—and I mean really sure—you can trust her, don't tell her about the money. It's not like you two are dating or getting married and she needs to know. This is a unique situation."

A unique situation. He couldn't argue with that. But his heart kept prodding him about misleading her.

"Thanks, Ed. It's good to hear your voice again."

"Same here. Call me anytime. I'll contact you when everything is ready." He hung up, and Dylan stared at the blank screen for a moment.

Ed's advice was good. It echoed his own thoughts since finding out the baby existed. But he hated lying to Gabby. She was big on truth and trust.

Was it so bad to let her believe he was a cowboy for hire? For a few more weeks?

If he told her now and she started fawning over him because she thought she could profit from it, he didn't know if he could handle being disillusioned again. He couldn't imagine her doing that, but what he could imagine was her reaction if he told her he'd inherited a fortune. She made no secret of the fact she didn't think much of guys who lived off their daddy's money.

Besides, if he spilled the beans, he would have no reason to be a cowboy. He was working on Stu's ranch because she didn't want Phoebe around a deadbeat. His millions made that point as dead as the deer carcass he'd stumbled across this morning while checking on a few cows.

The charade would have to continue—at least until the trust fund and child support papers were ready. It wasn't really harming anybody, him keeping his wealth a secret. He didn't need to feel guilty.

The longer he stayed, the more he wanted to be a regular part of Phoebe's life. He didn't want to only send gifts and cards occasionally. He wanted to be the uncle she could rely on as she grew older. What that looked like, he couldn't say at this point. Maybe coming into town every three months to visit or…

Images of him living in Rendezvous, riding horseback, fly-fishing, maybe even having a barbecue in the park with a group of friends flitted through his mind.

No, this wasn't a permanent thing. Just because Gabby was softening toward him didn't mean anything. Sure, he was attracted to her and thought she was doing a great job as a mom. But they came from different backgrounds. She was more grounded than he was. What would she think if she knew how aimless his traveling had been all last year? She'd be disappointed in him and think it was a waste of time and money to travel with no purpose. And she'd be right.

"There's no way I can work for Nolan." Gabby tucked her feet under her body on the comfy couch in the screened-in porch off Eden's living room Friday night. She'd always loved the Pages' ranch. The rambling white farmhouse had large windows and gorgeous views of the prairie and mountains. The sun was going out with a bang by streaking pinks and purples throughout the sky. Phoebe played with a toy on a fluffy rug between where Gabby and Eden sat on padded wicker chairs.

"I don't blame you." Eden's glass of iced tea sweated water droplets down its side. "He's always so…"

"Full of himself? Arrogant?" Gabby fluttered her eyelashes innocently.

Eden snickered. "I was going to say clueless, but those fit, too."

"Today I spent eight hours with him questioning my every move." Irritation bubbled up her core. It had been a bad day. "And it wasn't because he genuinely wanted to learn anything. He's convinced he has a better way to do everything. *Everything.*"

"Why would he think that? He's in the shipping business, not hotels." Eden took another sip.

"Exactly. If it wasn't the email system we use, it was the employee uniforms. And he had so many opinions on how the rooms should be organized and how he'd remodel them. Frankly, I agree they need to be remodeled, but the stuff he was suggesting sounded horribly out-of-date. Like, hire a designer already."

Phoebe began to babble. She was trying to stuff a purple plastic cow in her mouth. Every time she squeezed it, the cow made a mooing noise. Gabby returned her attention to Eden.

"If he stayed all day, does that mean he's already negotiating with Babs?" Eden asked.

"I don't know, and I'm too afraid to ask her."

"Well, there must be another job you could do here in town if he does buy the place."

Gabby slumped. "That's the problem—I love my job. And I want to work at the inn. Unless I take a big cut in pay, the only thing I can come up with is getting my insurance license, and it would mean I'd have to take classes and pass exams. But at least I'd have regular hours."

"You sitting behind a desk selling insurance?" Eden made a sour face. "Are there even any openings in town?"

"Who knows? Cathy Davies has worked the front desk forever at Dalton Insurance. She could put in a good word for me."

"Are there any other options?" Eden frowned.

She shrugged. "I'm just telling you what I've come up with, and it isn't much at this point."

"Maybe Nolan wouldn't be around much. It's not like he lives in Rendezvous."

The thought lifted her spirits. "Maybe you're right. He still works for his dad. It's not as if he's quitting his day job. At least, I hope not."

"Ba-ba-ba." Phoebe had shifted to all fours. She reached for a stuffed elephant, but it was too far away. She planted one hand forward.

"Look!" Gabby kept her voice soft. "Do you think she'll crawl?"

"Oh, I hope so!" Eden brought her hands together and watched Phoebe shift one knee ahead.

Gabby quickly got out her phone and scrolled through to take a video. Phoebe moved her other hand, her knee, and repeated the process. She crawled forward until she got to the elephant. And Gabby got it all on video.

"Good job, Phoebe!" Gabby clapped her hands. "You did it. You crawled."

Eden stretched out an open palm to Gabby, and they high-fived.

Phoebe gripped the elephant in one hand and flopped to a seated position. Then she chewed on the elephant's leg. Gabby couldn't help herself—she scooped up the baby and showered her with kisses. Phoebe cooed, then started to fuss, so she put her back on the floor to play with her toy.

"I wish Allison could have been here to see this," Gabby said as she sat back down. Her chest felt tight with emotion. She wanted the baby to reach these milestones, but each milestone hurt, knowing her sister was missing every one of them.

"I wish she could be here, too." Eden grew pensive. "Noah turned four a few months ago, and when he blew out the candles, I almost started crying because Mia will never see him grow up."

"Does it get easier?" She looked into Eden's brown eyes. They'd both lost sisters. Eden had helped raise Noah until Mason remarried a few weeks ago, so she knew what it was like to love her sister's child, too.

"It was easier when I took care of him." Eden turned away abruptly. "I knew life would change—it couldn't stay the way it was forever. Even if Mason hadn't remarried, Noah would continue to get older, go to school—he wouldn't need his auntie Eden anymore."

"He'll always need his auntie Eden."

"Not in the same way. Not like he used to. And that's okay, because he has a wonderful mommy in Brittany."

She'd known Eden was struggling, but her own grief and being thrown into instant motherhood had prevented her from thinking too much about Eden's pain.

"You know you can have your own family, right?" Gabby watched for her reaction.

"I suppose." Her voice sounded faraway as she gazed out the screened window. "Don't laugh, but I always saw myself being a ranch wife living here in Rendezvous—on this ranch, preferably."

"There are eligible ranchers here, you know." She kept her tone light.

"I know. But I'm not going to kid myself. The guys around here aren't really my type. Judd Wilson is quieter than me, and that's saying something. Cash McCoy is too wild. It would never work."

"Maybe you should get to know them better. They might surprise you."

Phoebe crawled to the side of the couch and pulled herself up to a standing position. Gabby picked her up and set her on her lap. She snuggled into her arms.

"Right back at you." Eden cast her a sly glance.

Her? Date? She shook her head. "I'm too busy. I have a million problems, and I'm not adding a potential boyfriend to the list."

"What about Dylan? He's good-looking. I've seen him a few times in town."

Jealousy flared hot and sudden. Did Eden want to date Dylan? Picturing him with Eden—or anyone else for that matter—brought a sour taste to her mouth. But who was she to object? This was her best friend, and if anyone deserved a great guy, it was Eden.

Was Dylan a great guy?

She hated to admit it, but he was growing on her.

He stopped by when he said he would. He'd gotten a job and seemed to really like it. He called or texted to arrange to see the baby, and he hadn't shown up unannounced since moving here.

"You got awfully quiet." With a gleam in her eye, Eden cocked her head.

"So far Dylan has been reliable, and he seems decent. If you want to date him, I can give you his number."

"Me?" Eden's face recoiled in horror. "No, I meant you. You should date Dylan."

At the thought of dating him, hope and anticipation did a happy dance around her heart. He was gorgeous. And easy to be with. And good with the baby.

And a cowboy.

Her number one deal breaker.

Even if she could get past his profession, she hadn't spent enough time with him to deem him worthy.

"No." Gabby shook her head. "Not going to happen."

"It's the cowboy thing, isn't it?" Her face fell.

"Yep."

"Couldn't you make an exception?"

She wouldn't answer. Because part of her wanted to make an exception. The same part of her had wanted to believe the best in her dad and Carl. It was her weakness and had let her down time and again. "No, I don't have room in my life for dating right now."

"I have too much room...for everything." Eden rested her head against the back of the chair. "Maybe you're right and I should get to know the guys around here better. I could even...try dating. I don't think Judd or Cash or any guy in town even knows I exist."

"What are you talking about?" She shook her head. "You're so beautiful and kind. They've noticed."

"Oh yeah? Then why haven't any of them asked me out? The only girls who get noticed around here are Stella Boone and Misty Sandpiper."

"Well…" Her words held a nugget of truth. "It's probably because Stella and Misty are around them more. They make an effort, do things with the guys."

"I don't want to do things with them."

Gabby studied her friend. It would do Eden good to get out and have some fun. She'd been more and more pensive lately.

"Why don't we organize a group outing. A barbecue or something? We can invite a bunch of people. Then it won't be awkward or weird."

"It will still be awkward and weird." Eden grimaced.

"No, it won't. You'll see. We can plan it for next week—Saturday. We'll have a picnic at the city park. Potluck. I'll spread the word." She perked up thinking about it. "Tomorrow at church you can personally invite Judd. I'll tell Stella to invite Cash and Misty and the other guys. Nicole can come. And Brittany and Mason."

"I guess a picnic would be fun." Worry lines creased Eden's forehead. "Could *you* ask Judd, though?"

"I think you should ask him."

"Then you'll have to invite Dylan."

"Fair enough." She instantly pictured Stella flirting with him, and Misty probably would, too. *Yuck.* They'd be all over him. And he'd eat up the attention. Carl always had.

Was it fair to keep comparing Dylan to Carl, though? When she was growing convinced he was nothing like her ex?

So what? It didn't mean he was fair game for her to date him. He was Phoebe's uncle. She'd be dealing with him the rest of her life. A botched romance wouldn't just hurt her, it would hurt Phoebe. She wouldn't do that to the baby.

Dylan may have overdressed for church. He glanced around at the people making their way down the aisle and regretted wearing a button-down shirt and tie. All the other men wore short-sleeved shirts open at the collar or polo-style shirts with jeans. His fitted dark gray dress pants had been overkill, too.

Yesterday, he'd driven to Jackson to buy supplies. He'd wanted to invite Gabby and Phoebe, but she'd made it clear Saturdays were her day to relax. He hadn't wanted to ruffle her feathers. Plus the conversation with Ed had forced him to do some thinking—not only about Gabby, but about his future, too.

Living in Texas didn't make sense if he wanted to see Phoebe on a regular basis. In fact, living in Texas didn't appeal to him at all now that Dad and Sam were gone. With the company sold, he had no place of employment. His friends had moved on without him, and he couldn't think of a reason to go back.

Yesterday, he'd been sure he'd feel in his element in Jackson since it was full of trendy restaurants and upscale shopping. And in some ways he had. He'd been raised to enjoy expensive boutiques and gourmet food; he was used to not checking a price tag and never thought twice about buying items he didn't really need.

But the things he needed the boutiques didn't carry. He was desperate for a fan and a coffeemaker, not the several-hundred-dollar espresso maker the kitchen store carried. He wanted towels strong enough to hold up to the dirt he brought in every night instead of the fluffy white hotel-quality ones he'd briefly considered purchasing.

He'd ended up dropping a lot of money on new clothes, including his current outfit, and now he wished he hadn't. These clothes didn't work in Rendezvous.

He didn't fit into his old life anymore, and he didn't seem to fit into the new one, either.

Maybe he was kidding himself that he could stay here for a month.

Clasping his hands and bowing his head, he tried to push away the feeling of defeat.

*God, what am I doing here? I'm pretending to be something I'm not. But I think I was pretending to be someone else back in Texas, too. What am I supposed to do?*

He straightened as he sensed someone wanting to enter the pew. Glancing up, he did a double take. Gabby smiled at him. Phoebe wore a pink dress and matching headband with an enormous bow. The baby's little nose scrunched as she grinned. He scooted down so they could sit.

"Can I help you with that?" He gestured to the diaper bag slung over her shoulder.

"No, I've got it."

He caught a whiff of her floral perfume. The baby held her hands out to him, and he gladly hauled her onto his lap, facing him. She clapped her palms against his cheeks and giggled. This kid—she brought so much joy to his heart. He puffed up his cheeks and she smacked them, laughing and loving every minute of it.

"You looked lonely over here," Gabby said when he'd gotten settled. "We figured we'd join you."

"I'm glad you did." He didn't care if she'd sat here out of pity or not; he welcomed her friendly face. Her blue sundress brought out her feminine side. She didn't wear much makeup, and she didn't need to. Her natural beauty called to him.

He ran a finger under his collar. What was going on with him? This was Phoebe's aunt, not a potential girlfriend. He had to do a better job of fighting this attraction. At least it seemed to be one-sided on his end at this point. The thought should have relieved him, but instead it was depressing.

Organ music played, and Gabby took Phoebe back into her arms. He followed the service and peeked at his niece and her pretty aunt often throughout. The pastor spoke about temptation. Dylan focused straight ahead. Temptation sat next to him and smelled fantastic.

Soon they were saying the final prayer and being ushered out of church. Gabby dropped her bulletin as they made their way down the aisle, and Dylan bent to pick it up for her. Handing it back, his fingers brushed hers, and his skin heated at the touch.

As they followed the crowd outside and down the sidewalk, he caught himself wanting to take her arm, hold her hand, keep her close to him. But he didn't have that right. So he stayed by her side, his spirits dropping, knowing his time with her today was about to end.

"What are you doing next Saturday?" She kept a tight hold on Phoebe, who was trying to bounce on her hip.

"Nothing, why?"

"Eden and I are organizing a picnic, and we want you to come. It's potluck. At the city park."

"I'd like that." He knew he was grinning like a fool and didn't care. A picnic. He'd been dreaming of one since he'd arrived. And if she was okay with him coming to a picnic, maybe she'd be okay with him asking her to go shopping with him, too. It couldn't hurt to ask, could it? "Can I ask for some advice?"

Her eyes sparkled with curiosity. "Of course."

"I need to buy some supplies, and I'm not sure where to go. I'm talking things like a fan and towels."

"There's a supercenter an hour south of here. It would be your best option."

"Okay. Thanks." If he asked her to come, would she say no?

"When are you going?" She adjusted Phoebe's head-band.

"I was thinking today. Why? Do you want to come with me?" He held his breath. He'd never been this insecure around a woman before. What was his problem?

"Yeah, I would. Phoebe is outgrowing her clothes, and I haven't had a chance to get down there to stock up on stuff."

She wanted to come with him. He stood taller. This day was looking up.

"What time do you want to leave?" he asked. The sooner the better in his opinion.

"Well, I'm going to try to spread the word about the picnic now, then I'll go home and change."

"I need to change, too." He stared down at his outfit and shook his head again.

"What was that look for?" Her mischievous smile made his pulse quicken.

"I wasn't sure what to wear." He shrugged.

"You look good to me."

She thought he looked good? His chest expanded. How about I pick you up in an hour?"

"I'll be ready." She flashed him a grin and disappeared in the crowd.

Rocking back on his heels, he wanted to pump his fist in the air, but instead he shoved his hands in his pockets and strolled toward the parking lot. Score one for team Kingsley. He'd gotten Gabby to agree to spend the entire afternoon with him.

Why was that a good thing? She didn't want to date him. And he couldn't really date her. Not as things stood, at least.

He and Gabby were friends, and outside of Stu, she was the only friend he had at the moment. He'd take whatever time she was willing to give.

As he reached his truck, he thought back to last week when yearning for the simple pleasures of a small town had practically knocked him over.

He was getting what he'd wished for. A community. Barbecues with friends. A purpose working on the ranch.

Sure, none of it would last, but he'd enjoy it while he could. Life had given him enough lemons lately. He'd happily drink the lemonade until it ran out.

# Chapter Seven

Something wasn't adding up about Dylan Kingsley. The man pushing the shopping cart next to her was more complicated than she'd originally thought. Or maybe she was the one complicating things.

On the ride here, they'd enjoyed a pleasant conversation. He'd told her about the summer he'd learned how to ride a horse. She'd filled him in on how she and Allison entertained each other as kids by running through sprinklers in the summer and playing house or Barbies. She'd asked him questions, but he'd been tight-lipped and vague about the rest of his childhood. It reminded her of when she'd first met him—and her suspicions had flared all over again. Had she been wrong about him? Was he hiding something from her? Was he really like Carl and she'd been fooling herself?

If he was like Carl, he'd fill up the cart and pretend he'd lost his wallet.

Phoebe was strapped into the cart and happily gripped the bar, watching everyone who walked by. Several people waved to her and mentioned what a cute baby she was. Their kind words warmed Gabby's heart.

# LOYAL READER
# REE BOOKS VOUCHER

**YES! I Love Reading, please send me up to 4 FREE BOOKS and Free Mystery Gifts from the series I select.**

Just write in "YES" on the dotted line below then return this card today and we'll send your free books & gifts asap!

➡️ _ YES _ ⬅️

Which do you prefer?

☐ **Love Inspired Romance®**
Larger Print
122/322 IDL GNQS

☐ **Love Inspired Suspense®**
Larger Print
107/307 IDL GNQS

☐ **BOTH**
122/322 & 107/307
IDL GNQ4

| | |
|---|---|
| FIRST NAME | LAST NAME |

ADDRESS

| | |
|---|---|
| APT.# | CITY |

| | |
|---|---|
| STATE/PROV. | ZIP/POSTAL CODE |

BUSINESS REPLY MAIL
FIRST-CLASS MAIL    PERMIT NO. 717    BUFFALO, NY

POSTAGE WILL BE PAID BY ADDRESSEE

READER SERVICE
PO BOX 1341
BUFFALO NY 14240-8571

NO POSTAGE
NECESSARY
IF MAILED
IN THE
UNITED STATES

"Where should we head to first?" Dylan asked.

"What do you need?" A blast of air-conditioning, bright fluorescent lights and displays of beach towels and plastic dishes greeted them as they passed the grocery section into a general merchandise area.

He listed the items, and she pointed to the far corner where housewares were located. "This way."

They found the fans. Gabby began checking the prices of each, and Dylan zoomed to a top-of-the-line model and hauled it into the back of the cart.

"Aren't you going to look at all of them?" She pointed to a cheap box fan.

"Why?" His thick eyebrows drew together, giving him an adorably confused look.

"To find the best value."

"This has the features I want." He dusted off his hands and joined her at the front of the cart.

"How do you know the other ones don't?"

"Box fans only blow in one direction." He nodded to the one she'd been looking at.

"It's inexpensive, though." Had he even checked the price?

"I'm sure it is, but it doesn't have what I need." He pointed to the other fans on the shelves. "Those two are basically the same model, and I'd have to buy an end table for them to sit on. The one I'm buying stands up, oscillates and has a remote control."

It sounded fancy and pricey. But she reluctantly conceded his argument made sense.

He resumed pushing the cart until they reached the bedding section.

A fluffy comforter in the palest mint green drew her eye. She sighed longingly. She didn't have the funds to

replace her current faded denim coverlet, but if she did
she'd go with the mint-green one. It was light. Feminine.

Dylan, on the other hand, was holding a navy-and-
tan bed-in-a-bag set at eye level to read what was in it.
She peeked at an identical one sitting on the shelf. The
price seemed terribly high. Trying to act nonchalant and
staying within reach of Phoebe, she eyeballed the prices
of the other comforters and bedspreads. He'd picked the
most expensive one. Surely, he'd put it down and find
another. But he didn't. He put it in the cart.

Her initial impressions from last weekend roared
back. The expensive truck. The small inheritance he
seemed to be blowing through like the wind. The way
he spent his money wasn't any of her business, but what
if it became her business? What if he used his relationship with Phoebe to try to borrow money from her?

She almost snorted. The idea was laughable. He
didn't strike her as the type. Really, she had to give
him the benefit of the doubt instead of letting her past
mistakes color all of her opinions about men.

"You mentioned towels." She used her most pleasant
tone. "Do you want to find them next?"

"Yeah." The corner of his mouth twisted. "Wait. The
bedding set—I'm not sure if it's the right one."

"Why not?" *Because it's over a hundred dollars!*

"It comes with a bunch of things I don't think I need."

"Like what?" She perked up. Was he asking her opinion?

He picked up the bedding set again and read. "Shams
and a bed skirt and a valance. I don't even know what
those things are."

"Shams are the fancy pillowcases you cover a pillow with and set on top of your regular pillows, the bed

skirt hides what's under the bed and a valance is like a minicurtain."

He grimaced and shoved the bedding set back on the store shelf. "Did you see any other sets without all that stuff? Nothing froufrou. Dark would be best."

"No pink stripes?" She winked as she pointed to a little girl's set a few feet away.

"For Phoebe, yeah. For me? No." His grin sent her heartbeat sprinting. "I'd get it dirty and ruin it."

Phoebe let out a cry and pounded on the bar, so Gabby unstrapped her and carried her down the aisle to check the other sets. "What about this? It comes with a set of sheets, two pillowcases and a lightweight comforter."

"Perfect. Dark gray. No polka dots or flowers. I like it." He stood behind her, looking over her shoulder. His cologne or aftershave reminded her of the mountain air—fresh and clean. If she took the tiniest step back, she'd be touching him.

She stiffened. No need to think about touching him. Instead, she pivoted forward so he could see the package better. "And the price is half the other one."

"Right." He read the description on the package. "But do you think it will hold up?"

"I do. More expensive doesn't always mean better quality."

"I'll take your word for it." He placed the bedding in the cart.

Twenty minutes later they'd added towels, cleaning products and a coffeemaker to the pile. She'd questioned his need for the more expensive coffeemaker, but he'd assured her it was necessary for the early-morning work he did. Did a cheap coffeemaker produce an inferior cup of coffee? She didn't know. She'd only ever had the cheapest model, and her coffee tasted fine.

As she glanced at the cart, she couldn't shake the worry that he was a spendthrift. What would he do when his money ran out?

Her dad had taken to driving a truck and preying on weak women in different towns. Carl had done the same, minus driving big rigs.

She didn't know what Dylan would do, and she really didn't want to find out.

All she knew was a man who wasn't responsible with his money wasn't the man for her.

Dylan couldn't believe how cheap everything was in this store. It was his first time shopping in a supercenter. His watch alone had cost ten times more than the contents of the entire cart. There was an extra spring in his step as they moseyed toward the baby section.

He wanted to buy some things for Phoebe. Spoil his niece a little bit. He got the impression Gabby wouldn't like it, though.

It was strange to have someone judging him for thinking he was spending too much on items he considered practically free. It reinforced his previous misgiving that Gabby had to worry about money in a way he never did. Shouldn't he be fast-tracking the trust fund and child support? For her sake?

She stopped and began browsing through a rack of baby clothes. Bright-eyed and quiet, Phoebe sat on her hip. One by one, Gabby selected sleeveless dress sets with tiny matching shorts ruffled at the legs. And one by one, she set them back after checking the price.

"What about this one?" He held up a baby blue dress

with bows on the back and a matching headband. It was cute. Phoebe would look adorable in it.

"I'm not sure." Gabby flushed, shaking her head. "I want to see what else they have before I make a decision."

He checked the tag. Under twenty bucks. Size 12 months. He furrowed his eyebrows together. Phoebe was nine months old. Would it be too big? "What size is she?"

"She's growing out of her 6–9 months clothes. That's the next size up." She shifted to the next circular rack and browsed through little T-shirts that snapped at the bottom.

"What all does she need?" He tossed the baby blue dress in the cart and reached for one with watermelon slices printed all over it.

"Onesies. A few dresses. Short outfits. Oh, and a hat. I've got to protect her head from the sun."

"I'm on it." He puffed out his chest and searched the area for shorts.

"Um, I've got this." Her eyes flashed with worry.

"I'm getting her some clothes." He wasn't budging. "She's my niece, too."

"Well…" She dragged the word out. "Don't buy much. You already have a lot to pay for." She nodded toward the cart.

He almost laughed. She was worried about him paying for all this stuff? It was a drop in the bucket. Nothing. "Don't worry. I've got it."

"I know it's none of my business but your inheritance… It won't last forever." Her eyes grew wide as if she couldn't believe she'd just said that. "I mean, it's always smart to save for a rainy day. Then if you get the itch to move around again, you won't have to worry about your money running out."

He averted his eyes, overcome with sudden emotion and insight. She wasn't judging him. She was worried. Worried he wouldn't be able to pay for everything, that he'd run out of money if he wasn't careful.

Shame rushed from his head to his toes in a big whoosh. He should tell her he was rich. It was wrong to mislead her and allow her to keep thinking whatever it was she thought.

What did she think?

"Why do you think my money will run out?" He crossed over to where she suddenly grew very interested in those baby T-shirt things.

Her neck grew pink and she didn't meet his eyes. "You've been doing… I don't know…this and that for the past year, and you mentioned a small inheritance. If you didn't have a job, you had to be spending it. And it costs a lot to live. The nest egg won't last forever."

"I was traveling. I went overseas." He couldn't bring himself to admit he'd been hopping from country to country, living in luxury, fine dining every night, watching the sun, moon and stars from expensive balconies and contemplating the meaning of life.

He hadn't figured out the meaning. And those twelve months seemed shamefully indulgent now that he'd met Gabby.

She raised her eyebrows. "Overseas. Traveling. Not cheap."

The truth climbed up his throat, ready to be spoken.

But he already knew how she'd react. And it wouldn't be to fawn over him and try to get money for herself.

She'd be disappointed in him.

Just like his father had always been.

"I never buy anything I can't afford." He tightened his jaw. It was true. And he was buying Phoebe some clothes. He didn't care if Gabby approved or not. She had no right to look down on him for his financial situation—whether she thought he was rich or poor. It was his business. Not hers.

He went back to the display table with itty-bitty shorts and selected half a dozen in various colors. Then he picked out T-shirts to match, threw four more dress sets in for good measure and selected a turquoise one-piece swimsuit with pink flamingos and ruffles.

A touch on his arm made him flinch and turn.

"Hey, I'm sorry." Gabby's pretty gray eyes swam with regret. "You're right. It's none of my business how you spend your money. I shouldn't have said anything."

He blinked twice as his heart swelled. "It's okay."

"No, it's not." Her throat worked as she swallowed. "I had a few complicated relationships. My father, in par-ticular, did things that made me not trust him, and my ex-boyfriend piled onto my trust issues. It was wrong of me to project their mistakes onto you."

He tilted his head, viewing her through new eyes. What had her father done to abuse her trust? And what about the ex? Had he broken her heart?

"I have trust issues, too, Gabby," he said quietly. "Why don't we finish up here and call it even?"

"Sounds good." Her genuine smile could have knocked him over with a feather.

As she walked back to the baby racks, an uncomfort-able feeling spread throughout his body.

He cared about her opinion.

He cared about her.

He hadn't cared about anyone since Sam and Dad died. He preferred it that way. Life was safer without responsibilities, but was it better? He wasn't sure he wanted to find out.

Gabby couldn't stop peeking at Dylan all the way home. They'd finished their shopping—she'd done a double take at his enormous bill but kept her mouth shut—and stopped at a nearby coffee shop for a snack and to give Phoebe her bottle before heading back. At the coffee shop, he'd told her about some of the places he'd visited last year. She hadn't realized he was so adventurous. He made it sound easy, riding a train from Paris to the Alps.

She'd been out of the state only a handful of times. She couldn't imagine traveling around the world, especially by herself the way Dylan had. Hadn't he been scared? Worried about not speaking the language? Lonely? Homesick?

He must have had a larger inheritance than she'd originally assumed. She wanted to tell him to hang on to his money. Invest it. It was nice of him to buy Phoebe some clothes, but she'd rather see him save for his future.

There she went again, assuming she knew everything about him. Who was she to conclude he didn't save? He could have a 401(k) tucked away and everything.

Casting a glance at his tanned arms lightly gripping the wheel, then up to his handsome profile and the T-shirt hugging his biceps, she mentally rolled her eyes at herself. *Sure, he's got a 401(k), a financial advisor and an accountant to boot.* Didn't all cowboys? She smiled at her own joke.

"What's the story on your dad?" He peered at her, keeping one eye on the road. The blue sky and green hills were empty and peaceful. "Or do you not want to talk about it?"

"I don't mind. My heart isn't so sore about it now." She thought back to the last time she'd seen him. Mom had kicked him out, and he'd been hauling his belongings out in trash bags. He'd come inside and reached for the framed family photo of the four of them, and Mom had swiped it out of his hand. *You ruined this family! You can't have the picture. It's mine!* And Gabby had glared at him, hating him for cheating on Mom. After her mother stormed out of the room, Allison had tiptoed to him and handed him the photo. He'd hugged her tightly while Gabby watched, her eyes burning with so much anger.

The anger had faded to a general wariness with time, but there was still a part of her that blamed him for destroying their family. He hadn't only cheated on Mom. He'd cheated on her and Allison, too.

"Dad was, for lack of a better word, charming," she said. "I thought the sun rose and set around him when I was a girl. He was gone a lot—working on local ranches or driving trucks—but whenever he was around, he made us feel special. Bought us toys, took us out for ice cream, that sort of thing."

"But?" He glanced her way, and she was relieved to see compassion in those brown eyes.

"But when he wasn't around, it was if we didn't exist. Mom did her best, but we were poor. It didn't bother me until I turned eleven. That's when I found out about the other women."

"He was cheating on your mom?" He frowned.

"Yes, with more than one lady. And the worst part was he was spending time with their children—more than he spent with us. All his charm and random gifts felt cheap and dirty after I found out."

Her throat felt raw. She'd thought she was over it, but talking about it brought a fresh wave of pain. She took a few deep breaths to calm her nerves. "Mom threw him out. I was angry at him. He came back a few times to visit, and Allison always wanted to see him, but I didn't. I couldn't forgive him for not only neglecting us, but for robbing us of our time with him so he could be with someone else's kids. It hurt."

"I can imagine," he said softly. "Do you ever talk to him?"

"No. And I don't talk much with my mom, either. After the divorce, she flitted from boyfriend to boyfriend like a lovesick teenager. It was as if when Dad left, she decided she no longer had responsibilities. Allison and I were basically raising ourselves."

"Now I know why you're so nurturing and responsible." The cleft in his chin drew her attention. He thought she was nurturing? Responsible? She tried not to let it go to her head.

She stared out the window. "What was your dad like? You must miss him."

"Sometimes I do." His knuckles tightened around the steering wheel. "And sometimes I think I'm looking for closure."

"Why? Weren't you close?"

"I wouldn't say close. I mean, we worked together, but he had high standards. It was difficult to live up to them."

"You worked together?" Finally she was learning

something concrete about his life before his brother and dad died.

His face flushed, and he waved like it didn't matter. "He owned a business. I worked for him. Then he sold it."

She had a feeling there were about a million things left unsaid between each short statement. "I take it you didn't want him to sell it?"

He met her eyes then. So much hurt was in them, she was tempted to reach over and touch his arm to comfort him.

"I didn't even know he wanted to sell it."

"He didn't ask you about it? Warn you in advance?" Her stomach clenched. It sounded mean. Needlessly hurtful.

"No," he said quietly, his gaze focused ahead. "I've blamed him. I've blamed myself. None of it changes anything. He's still gone."

"What type of business was it?"

"Can we not talk about it anymore?"

"Sure." A few miles sped by as questions piled up in her mind. It must have been hard on Dylan to find out secondhand his father was selling the company. Like her, he'd been betrayed by a parent. "What about your mother?"

He let out a half-hearted snort. "She was kind of like yours, except she used me to get back at my father. They divorced when I was three."

"What do you mean she used you?" Gabby knew people who refused to follow visitation schedules and made life as miserable as possible for their ex-spouses at the expense of their kids. One of her high school friends had developed an eating disorder because of her parents' drama.

"She'd fight him about when I could visit and demand more child support. She's had a few husbands since. Nothing really changes. We don't talk anymore."

"I'm sorry. I understand, but I'm still sorry."

"I am, too. I wish people didn't have to be so selfish sometimes. Your parents missed out on you, and it's a shame because you're a really great person."

"Thank you." The compliment warmed her like the summer sun. "It would be great if divorce didn't have to be so messy. I'm twenty-seven and still miss having parents to lean on."

"I know exactly what you mean." His lips curved into a soft smile. "We'll make sure Phoebe never feels like a chess piece or an afterthought."

*We'll?* What did he mean by that?

"Yes, I'll do my best to make her feel loved and important." She watched for his reaction.

"So will I."

"You will? Am I missing something? I thought you were staying here for a month or so." She tried to ignore the anxiety sizzling through her veins. If he'd changed his mind about staying, he could also change his mind about wanting a more active role—a legal role—in Phoebe's life. If he went to the courts, they'd probably agree.

"I am, and I'm not sure what I'm doing next, but I know it won't be in Texas. I'd like to be closer to Rendezvous, at least within driving distance, to see Phoebe more often. I don't want her to only know me through birthday cards and Christmas presents."

On the surface it made sense. He wasn't making

demands, just stating he wanted to see the baby on a regular basis. But Gabby had seen too much, had been lied to too many times to take his words at face value.

The words cowboys said sounded good, but their actions never matched up.

She'd been warming up to Dylan. She actually liked spending time with him. But she couldn't forget what was important—loving and protecting Phoebe. And to do that, she'd better start safeguarding her own heart before she went and made another stupid mistake like falling for Dylan Kingsley.

## *Chapter Eight*

The following Saturday afternoon, Dylan carried a cooler to the pavilion in the city park where a crowd had gathered. A strong wind from last night had mellowed to a gentle breeze, and sunshine made everything bright. Laughter and conversation grew louder as he approached. He couldn't believe two weeks ago he'd been watching other people hang out in this very park, and now here he was—getting ready to hang out with them, too. He might not belong here the way they all did, but he'd been invited. It was enough for now.

Enough for now? He scoffed. It would have to be enough for forever. He had no business making long-term plans here, considering no one knew the truth about him.

He wasn't like them.

He hadn't earned his money. He'd inherited it. And he'd let down the two people he'd loved the most. When Gabby found out the truth, he had a feeling he'd be letting her down, too.

*Stop being negative. What's the big deal? You're*

*rich. Who cares? Enjoy this. For once, just relax and enjoy a simple outing.*

He scanned the crowd for the cute, no-nonsense brunette who'd organized this shindig. There she was. Gabby's dark brown hair was pulled back into a high ponytail. Her white shorts showed off her trim figure, and her brick red tank top draped like a blouse to her hips. She was laughing at something someone said. He frowned when he saw who she was talking to. He'd seen the guy in church last week. Gabby seemed to be very friendly with him.

She turned and stared straight at Dylan. Time seemed to stop as their eyes met. Then hers crinkled in the corners as she grinned and waved him over. "Dylan, come meet everyone."

A flush of adrenaline spiked through his veins. How had he gotten so fortunate to meet this woman? She was going out of her way to make him feel welcome. And she did it without an ulterior motive, unlike some of the women from his past.

He strode under the pavilion and placed the cooler he'd borrowed from Stu in line with the other ones, then he wiped his hands down his shorts and made his way to Gabby's side.

"Dylan, this is my friend Mason Fanning." Gabby shifted to look up at him, then extended her arm to indicate the man she'd been talking to. "He's in my Tuesday night support group. And this is his new bride, Brittany."

Relief spread through his chest, and he probably pumped both Mason's and his beautiful wife's hands a little too hard.

"Gabby told us you lost your brother," Mason said.

"I'm sorry. It's terrible losing someone you love when they're so young."

This guy spoke as if he had experience with it. "Thank you, I appreciate it."

"You'll find several people, including myself, around here who have lost special people way too soon. If you need anything, I'm here."

He didn't know what to say. Another stranger going out of his way to welcome him. He didn't deserve this.

"Oh, there's Eden! I've been dying to introduce you." Gabby moved past him to greet her friend. He watched them hug. Gabby dragged her by the hand to him. The petite brunette had an understated beauty. "Dylan, this is Eden Page. She babysits Phoebe for me, and she's my best friend in the whole world."

"It's my pleasure." He smiled at her, wanting to put her at ease. A slight blush rose to her cheeks, and her kind eyes instantly made him like her. She was slightly taller than Gabby, with expressive brown eyes and shiny, dark brown hair that slid over her shoulders.

"It's good to meet you, too. I'm glad you found Gabby and the baby. Phoebe is such a sweet thing. I'm thankful she'll have an uncle."

"Mason, why didn't you tell me Ryder was coming?" Gabby's voice rose with excitement, and once again, she rushed away.

Dylan turned his attention back to Eden, but her face had lost some of its color. He peered into her eyes. "Hey, are you okay?"

"I'm fine." She didn't look fine.

"Why don't you sit down? I'll get you something to drink."

Her eyebrows formed a V, but she let him lead her to a picnic table.

"What can I get you? A Coke? Water?"

She sat on the bench and stared up at him. "Um, I don't need anything."

"There you are." Gabby appeared, dragging someone by the hand behind her. "For a minute I thought you guys ditched me."

Dylan shifted to introduce himself, but his mouth dropped open instead. Wasn't this Mason? The man he'd just met?

"Dylan, this is Ryder Fanning," Gabby said. "He's Mason's identical twin."

"Good to meet you." Ryder thrust out his hand, and Dylan shook it.

"Identical twin. I thought I was seeing double for a minute." He chuckled, shaking his head.

"Trust me, you're not the only one." Ryder grinned. "Mason and I didn't even know each other existed until last Christmas. It took us a while to get used to seeing each other."

"Really? You didn't know each other? I've got to hear this story." He glanced down at Eden quickly to make sure she wasn't going to pass out. Her color had returned, and her lips were pursed. She didn't seem thrilled to have Ryder around, but what did he know?

"Excuse me." Eden stood and gave them both a lukewarm smile. "I see someone I need to talk to."

Dylan stepped aside so she could leave, and then he turned his attention back to Ryder, but Ryder's attention was firmly fixed on Eden as she strode away.

"I'll be right back. I have to do something." Ryder followed Eden.

"That was weird." Gabby wore a thoughtful expression. "Oh, good. She's talking to Judd." She leaned closer to him. "She actually took my advice. I'm floored."

"Where's Phoebe?" It occurred to him he hadn't seen the little ball of cuteness, yet. He'd stopped in at Gabby's a few nights this week. She had even allowed him to give Phoebe her bottle and showed him how to change a diaper. He'd mangled the first one, and the second had fallen off when he'd picked up the baby, but the third had stayed put. It was a start.

"Babs insisted on watching her. She thinks I don't have enough fun, but she's wrong."

He hadn't considered how raising Phoebe had impacted Gabby's life. "Do you miss your life, you know, before raising the baby?"

"Oh no." She laughed, her teeth flashing as she grinned. "Life is much better now, well, except for Allison being gone. She would have loved this party."

He found it difficult to believe being plunged into motherhood with no help or warning would make anyone's life better. But Gabby wasn't the average woman, either.

"Hey, boss, introduce us to your friend." The flirtatious blonde he'd met the day he'd walked into the inn materialized with a tall, curvy girl who had light brown hair and hazel eyes.

Gabby stiffened. Was that a stifled groan? He must have been mistaken, because she smiled brightly. "Dylan, this is Stella Boone, you might remember her from the inn. We work together. And this is Misty Sandpiper."

Stella moved to his right side, and Misty somehow

edged to his other side, leaving Gabby standing awkwardly in front of them. Both girls began peppering him with questions, and Gabby raised her eyebrows, gave him a smirk and told him she'd be back in a little while. Disappointment broke his concentration, but he forced himself to engage with Stella and Misty.

As he answered their questions and admitted he was from Dallas, Stella clung to his arm and raved about how she always wanted to go there and how he'd have to take her sometime. He couldn't picture a scenario where he'd ever take Stella to Dallas, but he nodded politely, all the while keeping an eye on Gabby. A very pregnant woman hugged her, and the cowboy Eden had been chatting with tipped his hat to the pregnant woman. Eden disappeared down a path, and Ryder followed her a few minutes later. Mason had his arm slung over Brittany's shoulders when several guys broke away from the group to grill the burgers.

One of the men stopped to talk to Gabby. Dylan narrowed his eyes. The guy looked to be in his late twenties, and he was handsome, lean and muscular. Dylan could see the appreciative gleam in the guy's gaze clear over here, and the cowboy kept getting closer to Gabby. She laughed at whatever he said, and then he had the audacity to whisper something in her ear.

Dylan clenched his hands into fists.

"Don't you think so, Dylan?" Stella asked.

"What?" He had to pull it together. What was Stella talking about anyhow?

"We should plan a day trip to the hot springs soon."

"Oh, right. Sounds fun." It didn't sound fun, though, not unless Gabby was coming. "I'm real busy at the ranch. I don't know if I'll be able to get away."

"But you *have* to come with us. Stu won't mind if you play hooky one afternoon." She batted her eyelashes at him.

He wouldn't say it out loud, but the only woman he'd consider skipping out on the ranch for was Gabby. And from the looks of it, he wasn't the only cowboy in town who felt that way.

Where had Eden disappeared to? Gabby barely listened to Cash McCoy's tale of getting bucked off a bull at last weekend's rodeo. Eden was supposed to be making an effort with Judd Wilson, but Judd was standing silently near Nicole, who didn't seem bothered by the lack of conversation. And Eden was nowhere in sight.

How was she going to get Eden on a date if she was never around the guys who would date her?

The one person who would be guaranteed a date after the picnic was Dylan. The way the single ladies were fawning over him was getting annoying. She hadn't invited him here to jump-start his dating life. The only one she wanted to play matchmaker for was Eden.

She discreetly scanned the crowd and caught Dylan laughing at something Stella and Misty said. Those two had latched on to each of his arms like rabid nurses conducting earth's final blood drive. Seriously, didn't they have anyone else to talk to? They acted like he was a celebrity or something.

He was probably lapping up all the female attention. How long would it be before he was too busy to stop by and see Phoebe? She wouldn't think about it. Wasn't this what she wanted, anyhow? For him to get bored and move on so her life could go back to normal?

Well, it *had* been nice of him to bring over dinner

Tuesday and Thursday this week. He'd been as excited as she was when Phoebe crawled throughout the living room. And when she'd insisted on teaching him some of the basics of baby care, he'd taken her guidance like a champ. She wished she would have videotaped him changing Phoebe's diaper—it had been hilarious.

She frowned. Would she and Phoebe get shoved aside as afterthoughts when Dylan knew more people? Especially pretty girls like Stella and Misty? Her gaze tracked to where a small crowd of women had gathered around him.

It appeared he'd freed his left arm from Misty's claws and was attempting to loosen Stella's grip, as well. He stepped away from them. She wished she could hear what he'd said. Their disappointed faces soothed her irritation.

"Excuse me, Cash, but I think the guys are done grilling the burgers. I'm going to announce it's time to eat." She was glad to have an excuse to get away from him. Cash was exactly the kind of cowboy she avoided thinking about romantically—he knew he was good-looking, and he charmed every girl he came across.

"Everyone," she yelled, clapping her hands, "the food is done—" No one could hear her.

A high-pitched whistle got everyone's attention. Dylan's index finger and pinky were in his mouth as he whistled again. The pavilion grew quiet.

He approached her and grinned. "Thought you could use some help."

Her heart should *not* be singing a show tune right now.

"Thanks for coming, everyone," she said loudly. "Go ahead and get in line for the food—it's all ready."

"Mind if I say grace, Gabby?" Mason said before the conversations resumed.

"That would be terrific."

They all bowed their heads, and as soon as the short prayer was finished, a line formed at the tables covered with checkered tablecloths and filled with casseroles, salads, slices of watermelon and trays of cookies and cakes.

She loved potlucks. And picnics. And sunny days at the park surrounded by good friends.

"Should we get in line?" Dylan interrupted her reverie.

"Sure, but I understand if you'd rather eat with your fan club." She kind of hoped he would. Then her suspicions would be confirmed, and she could stifle some of the tender feelings she'd been having toward him.

"My fan club?" His face grew red. "Please don't ever leave me alone with them again."

"Why not?" Was he being serious? They fell into the back of the line.

"I feel more comfortable with you." His brown eyes gleamed with sincerity.

The compliment rushed through her, blowing down the house of cards guarding her heart.

Dylan preferred to be with her. He chose to be with her over younger, prettier women.

*Do you really believe it? It's a classic cowboy move. Make you think he prefers you to them, then go behind your back and flirt with them. As soon as we're done eating, he'll find an excuse to talk to them again.*

They filled their plates and took seats at a long picnic table. Mason and Brittany joined them. Then Ryder and Nicole, followed by Judd. Eden sat across from Judd.

Gabby bit into her burger. At least one thing was going right. Eden and Judd were having a conversation. Her friend even chuckled at something he said.

Gabby relaxed. She didn't need to get all amped up over nothing. Who cared if Dylan really did prefer her company to Stella's and Misty's? She had no interest in being more than friends. She'd be thankful she got along with him...for Phoebe's sake.

The next hour was filled with friendly conversation, way too many desserts, and then some of the guys drifted away to try their hands at horseshoes. The ladies found seats in the shade to chat while they watched.

"That's quite the hunky uncle Phoebe has." Brittany's eyes sparkled as she turned to Gabby. Her tone was all teasing. "Must be terribly hard to spend time with him."

"How long's he staying, Gabby?" Nicole turned to her, curiosity all over her face.

"I don't know." She sounded snippy and knew it. "If you'd like to take him off my hands and spend time with him, you're welcome to it."

They both raised their eyebrows with amused expressions and sat back.

"I thought everything was going okay with him." Eden watched her thoughtfully. "Did something happen?"

Her tension mellowed. What was wrong with her? These were her friends, and they were just having some fun.

"No, nothing happened. I'm sorry. It's just all new." It wasn't. Not really. The past two weeks had allowed her to get to know him better, and her gut was screaming he was a good guy. But was he?

It was too early to tell.

"Well, I give you a lot of credit for accommodating him," Brittany said. "I'm sure it hasn't been easy rearranging your schedule to let him get to know the baby."

Actually, it had been easy. Very easy. He'd made few demands, and had bent over backward to see Phoebe only when convenient to her.

"So you don't know how long he's staying in town?" Nicole asked. "Do you think he'll make it permanent?"

Hope zinged up her spine.

"I don't know. I don't think he knows his plans yet." But if he did stay… She pictured outings together like last week's shopping expedition, and more walks by the river with Phoebe. Friday nights for pizza and catching up.

"Have you heard anything more about the inn?" Eden asked. "Has Nolan been back?"

"No to both." Good, a change in topic was desperately needed. "Apparently Nolan's been away on a business trip, and Babs said she's had a few nibbles but no bites."

"Well, that's good news, right?" Nicole asked.

"Yes, it buys me time."

"Oh, Eden—" Brittany whirled to face Eden "—do you think you'd have time this week to come over to the studio and look at the apartment above it with me? Mason insists it's time to renovate, and I agree, but I want a female opinion."

"I'd love to." Eden's face lit up.

They got out their phones and checked their calendars. As Brittany and Eden discussed the layout of the apartment above Brittany's dance studio, Gabby watched the horseshoe game. Mason and Ryder were

artners, and Dylan and Judd were the other team. The
link of metal on metal and a round of female cheers
on the other side of the horseshoe pit told her someone
had scored.

As Stella and Misty high-fived each other and cheered
for Dylan, Gabby tried not to get annoyed. Dylan wasn't
hers. Not even close. And she had dating rules.

No cowboys. Especially good-looking ones.

She needed to douse these feelings—the attraction
and the jealousy—pronto. Nothing good would come
from them.

Dylan couldn't remember the last time he'd spent an
afternoon with such welcoming people. Mason had invited him to stop by the ranch anytime. Judd had been
quiet, but he'd mentioned hunting together this fall. And
Ryder had peppered him with questions about being a
ranch hand after Dylan told him he didn't have a ton of
experience and that Stu was teaching him everything
he needed to know.

He hauled the cooler to the back of his truck, then
returned to the pavilion to help Gabby collect her dishes
and the camping chairs she'd brought.

"All set?" He slung the folded chairs in their bags
onto his shoulder.

"I can get them. You don't need to help." She carried a casserole dish in one hand and held out the other.

He ignored it. "I want to."

They made their way to her car, and he waited for
her to pop the trunk before setting the chairs inside.
She stowed the dish in there as well, then straightened
and slammed it shut.

"What are you doing now?" he asked.

"Picking up Phoebe from Babs's place." Her gray eyes gleamed with attitude. He wasn't sure why.

"Want some company?" He hoped she understood he meant he wanted to be with her, not just to see the baby.

"Why? Are you lonely? Stella would be happy to hang out with you." A sarcastic smile briefly lifted her lips.

"I would never be that lonely." He couldn't help noticing they were only a few inches apart. He instinctively wanted to close the gap. "I had a good time today, and I don't want to go back to the sauna yet."

"The sauna?"

He chuckled. "Yeah, I've named my cabin the sauna. It's about the same size as one, and it's definitely the same temp."

"Really? Even with the new fan?" She leaned against her car. "I thought you were a big, strong cowboy. Aren't you supposed to be immune to the weather?"

"You're thinking of a Navy SEAL. I'm a mere man."

"I suppose you could come over for a while—to enjoy my air-conditioning." She brought her index finger to her lips, not meeting his eyes. "Give me fifteen minutes to pick up Phoebe and meet me at my place."

"Done." He opened her car door and waited for her to slide into the driver's seat. Then he bent slightly and tried to find the words he wanted to say.

She looked up at him with a confused expression.

"Thanks. For inviting me today. For letting me come over now." He straightened and shut her door before she could respond.

*Idiot.* He didn't know what he'd wanted to say, but it wasn't *thanks for inviting me.*

He marched back to his truck, only to be waylaid by Stella and Misty.

"We're going to Rendezvous Saloon tonight." Stella acted coy. "Why don't you join us?"

The last thing he wanted to do was go to some bar with these two. "Uh, no, thanks." He gave them a smile. "I have plans."

And he waved to them, got into his truck and slowly backed out.

He had Gabby to thank for that—he had her to thank for everything. Raising his niece. Getting him a job. Introducing him to her friends. Making him feel like he belonged here.

He'd find a way to repay her.

The trust fund and child support came to mind.

*Not yet.*

But he'd have to do it soon.

## Chapter Nine

She'd messed up. She shouldn't have told Dylan to stop by.

Gabby set the empty casserole dish in her sink and filled it with hot water. Phoebe had fallen asleep on the way home from Babs's place, and Gabby had left her strapped in her car seat on the living room floor. Dylan would be here any minute. What had possessed her to tell him to come over?

Flattery. That's what.

He'd made it clear he preferred her company to Stella's and Misty's, and instead of being rational and reminding herself they were mere words, she'd clung to them. And she shouldn't have. He was her friend. Nothing more. And she'd make doubly sure to keep it that way.

She couldn't rely on Dylan. If she started leaning on him, getting close to him… It would only leave her with hurt feelings or worse.

A knock on the door set her heartbeat off on a mad dash. Taking a deep breath, she forced herself to keep her pace slow as she approached the door and opened it.

Dylan held two iced coffees in his hands. "Thought

you might need one of these. Hope you like caramel macchiatos."

"Ooh, they look great. Thanks." She stepped aside to let him in. His arm brushed her shoulder, and she was all too aware why the ladies had flocked to him at the picnic. He had a presence. He didn't need to flirt for attention. He automatically got it. "Make yourself at home."

"This is *much* better than the lumpy sofa at my place." His knees splayed and legs sprawled as he got comfortable on the couch. He'd taken off his running shoes, and somehow made the shorts and T-shirt look even better than his formal church outfit—and that had been appealing indeed. "Is your coffee okay? I wasn't sure if you liked the sweet stuff."

She'd already slurped a long drink and practically swooned at the frozen deliciousness. She took a seat on the chair near the couch and kicked her feet up on the ottoman.

"I love the sweet stuff." She took a moment to study him. He looked more relaxed here than he had at the picnic, and that was to be expected. Meeting new people could be overwhelming. There was an air of contentment around him as if life didn't get much better than this.

As a matter of fact, she had a little of the same feeling, too.

"You had a good time today, didn't you?" She watched for his reaction.

His smile was instant and genuine. "Yeah, I did. Your friends are nice. I like them."

Pride filled her chest. Who didn't want to hear they had good taste in friends?

"I agree. They're great."

"So what was the deal with Eden and Ryder?" He sipped his iced coffee and watched her through those curious brown eyes.

"What do you mean?" She didn't think there was a deal between them—had she missed something?

He shrugged. "I don't know. I got the impression she doesn't like him much."

"Really?" She curled her legs to the side. "Why do you say that? She's never said anything to me."

It didn't surprise her Eden hadn't said anything negative about Ryder. She kept her opinions to herself. Gabby, on the other hand, spoke hers loudly and often.

"Maybe I'm wrong. She acted funny when he arrived, and it almost seemed like she was trying to avoid him, but he wasn't taking the hint. He followed her a couple of times."

"He did?" She hadn't considered Ryder and Eden could be on the outs. But why would they be? He wasn't even from around here. He lived in Los Angeles. Just because he'd been visiting more often didn't mean there was something going on between them she didn't know about.

"Yeah. But she was talking to that guy—the one in jeans and a cowboy hat."

He'd just described half a dozen guys there.

"Did he have short black hair? A slight gap in his teeth?"

Dylan lifted one shoulder. "I don't know. I didn't get a good look at him. It wasn't the jokey guy who was all over you. It was the quiet one."

Must have been Judd. And Cash had not been all over her. "Cash is friendly to all the ladies."

"He looked extra friendly when he was with you." The words were low, almost beneath his breath.

"Yeah, well, that's his way." She should be offended he was judging Cash, but she wasn't—in fact, she felt positively buoyant. Was he jealous?

"I know. I could tell you were trying to get away from him. Some people are hard to shake."

"Like Stella and Misty?" She blinked innocently.

"Yes. They aren't just hard to shake, they need to be professionally removed—like superglue or a termite infestation."

She laughed.

"Are you seeing any of those guys?" The question sounded light, but the gleam in his eyes told her otherwise.

"No."

"Why not?"

She dunked the straw into the coffee a few times. "I'm not into cowboys."

"And why's that?" He sank back into the couch, his expression serious.

Instead of automatically changing the subject, she stared at him. They'd shared personal stories before, but none this close to her heart. Telling him about Carl—not everything, obviously—might not be a bad thing. If he knew why she didn't date cowboys, he'd get the hint and know she wasn't interested.

"I told you about my dad." She set the drink on a coaster on the end table, steepled her fingers and brought them below her chin. "My ex also let me down."

"What did he do?" He leaned forward with his elbows on his knees.

"He wasn't who I thought he was. I was eighteen, a

senior in high school, planning a way for Allison and I to move out of Mom's trailer after I graduated, and Carl came along. He was older, tall, good-looking—a cowboy. All the girls crushed on him when he rode into town. And I couldn't believe he noticed me."

Dylan scowled.

"We started dating almost instantly. He said all the right things, and I lapped them up like the naive school-girl I was. Of course, I thought I was so smart and cool. I wasn't." She shrugged one shoulder in self-mockery. "I'd had a job at the grocery store since I turned six-teen, and I worked as many hours as possible outside of school to save for Allison and I to live on our own. Within a few weeks, Carl had a funny habit. He always needed me to pay for whatever we were doing. He'd claim he lost his wallet or had lent money to a friend. Soon he needed help paying for his gas or an overdue bill. He'd always look so embarrassed. I would give it to him. In my eyes he was perfect."

Dylan shifted but didn't speak.

"He always assured me he'd pay me back as soon as he got paid. I dated him for six months before I re-alized he wasn't faithful." She almost choked on the words. He'd been more than unfaithful; he'd been mar-ried to someone else. After all these years, the shame of it still felt fresh.

"I never saw a penny of my money again," she said. "It was a hard lesson to learn."

"Did you break up with him?"

"Yeah, but it took me a couple more weeks before I realized he wasn't going to change and he didn't really love me. Allison and I moved to Rendezvous not long after I graduated. We stayed with our grandma. Starting over in a new place helped a lot."

"Do you ever miss him?" Dylan asked gently. "Did you love him?"

The questions surprised her. Previously she would have said no, she hadn't loved him or missed him, but now that she was older, she could admit the truth. "Yes and yes. But also no and no."

He barked out a laugh and shook his head. "Well, what is it? Yes or no?"

"At first I missed him terribly. I was convinced I loved him. I thought he was the love of my life. I had wedding bells in my head. But after being away for a while, I realized I only missed who I thought he was, and that I'd fallen in love with a mirage, not a real person."

"Hmm…" He sat back again, staring ahead as if contemplating her words. "I never thought of it that way, but I know exactly what you mean."

"You do?" She hadn't expected him to understand. "What happened to you?"

"Robin. She and I met at a party of a mutual friend. She was smart, gorgeous and she wanted to talk to me. Like you, I was surprised she chose me. She was so friendly and outgoing. Soon, we were dating. I worked for my dad at the time."

"What did you do for him?" It was odd he would think a beautiful woman choosing him would be surprising. Didn't he know how handsome he was? And his undemanding personality drew people to him.

"Eh." He shrugged. "Mostly pushed papers around and made sure people were doing what they were supposed to."

"You weren't working on a ranch?" She'd never pictured him pushing papers and managing people.

"No, not at the time."

"What kind of company was it?"

He didn't meet her eyes. "It was in the energy field."

He seemed embarrassed. Maybe his dad hadn't been a very good businessman or something. She'd seen plenty of businesses come and go in Rendezvous.

His jaw clenched. "Anyway, Robin and I dated for several months. At first I liked her take-charge attitude. She made the plans. It was nice. Until she decided to take charge of my entire life. Everything was about getting ahead, meeting the right people. No matter what I did, it disappointed her. When I told her Dad sold the company, she left me."

Her spirits sank. She hadn't been the only one used and dumped.

"I tried to get her back, but she was done." His fingertips tapped against his shorts. "After my dad died, she suddenly came back into my life. She wanted to get back together—she was back to happy, friendly Robin. But it was because of the inheritance."

"Oh no, that's terrible!" Gabby pressed a hand over her chest. She thought back to when they'd first met, and she'd been convinced he was just another deadbeat cowboy. All because Carl had hurt her. How had Robin's treatment of him colored his first impression of her?

"I survived." He shrugged.

Phoebe made noises, alerting them she was waking up.

"She'll be hungry." Gabby got to her feet and headed to the kitchen to make a bottle.

"Do you mind if I turn on the Rockies game?" he asked. "If you had plans or something, though..."

"Go ahead. I don't mind. I like to keep up with the scores. People staying at the inn love talking sports." She actually enjoyed watching baseball games in the summer. Plus it seemed something friends would do—not romantic at all. And if he was going to be here, she might as well keep it as far from romance as possible. Now that he'd opened up to her about his ex and his previous job, she felt closer to him. It was fine if they were going to be semirelated through Phoebe, but it wasn't fine at all if she started to fall for him.

The sound of the television clicking on mingled with Phoebe's fussy sounds as Gabby prepared the bottle. Then the baby grew quiet. Gabby peeked around the cupboard, and her heart melted.

Dylan had gotten Phoebe out of the carrier and was cradling her to his chest. He bounced her gently, whispering something in her ear.

There was something about seeing a brawny man tenderly holding a baby that went straight to her heart.

Maybe watching baseball together wasn't a good idea.

*You're just lonely. This doesn't mean a thing.*

"Can I feed her?" He met her eyes as she approached him with the bottle.

It seemed a harmless request. Why was her stomach dipping in resistance?

"Sure, why not?"

He settled on the couch with Phoebe in his arms and began feeding her the bottle. Phoebe stared at him with laser-like intensity, and Gabby returned to her chair.

As she watched them, her eyes grew heavy. The

crack of the bats and drone of the announcers on television only lulled her more. She tried to stay awake, but it had been a long day. She'd close her eyes. Just for a minute.

The loud ringtone coming from Gabby's phone almost gave him a heart attack. He glanced over at her, curled up in the chair, sleeping. She looked young, beautiful and peaceful. He checked his own phone—after eleven o'clock at night. Should he try to wake her up?

He shifted Phoebe, also sleeping, to his other arm and reached over to shake Gabby's shoulder. "Hey, wake up. Someone is calling you."

She lifted her head, her eyelids trying to open, and gave him the most confused stare he'd seen in a while.

"What? Why are you here? Where am I?" Her voice was muffled as if she chewed on cotton. He tried not to laugh.

"You're at your apartment. You fell asleep."

Her phone blared again.

She bolted upright and swiped the phone. "Hello?"

Expressions of anxiety, then concern, then downright worry tightened her face.

"Okay, calm down. I'll be right there. No, you're not bothering me…Of course not. I'll come to you." She hung up.

"What's wrong?" he asked.

"It's Eden. She had some bad news and is completely freaking out. I've never—not once since I've known her—seen her get hysterical about anything." Gabby got up. Her jerky movements proved she wasn't quite awake all the way. "I have to go out there."

"Want me to go get her?" He stood, keeping Phoebe cradled under his arm.

"No, no. I'll go. You wouldn't know how to find her." She scurried to the kitchen, grabbed her keys and her purse, then smacked her forehead. "The baby."

"I'll take care of her. You go find your friend."

"No. I'll call Babs..." She rubbed her right eyebrow and shook her head. "I can't. I forgot she was going to Jackson after I picked up the baby. No big deal. Phoebe can come with me..." She seemed to be talking to herself.

"Gabby." He put his hand on her shoulder. "I will stay here and take care of Phoebe."

"You?"

Didn't she think he could handle it? Should he be offended? "Yes. After you fell asleep, I changed her diaper and played with her. We were fine then, and we'll be fine now."

"I don't know." She chewed on her fingernail.

"Look, she's sleeping." He nodded to the baby. "Why wake her?"

Her gray eyes softened. "I guess you're right. Her formula is in the kitchen. The bottles are in the cupboard. If she starts fussing, assume she's hungry. Make sure you burp her. And be prepared for a nasty diaper—it could blow right through her pajamas."

Nasty diaper? He did not look forward to that.

"Oh, you need to put her in her pajamas. Come on, I'll show you where everything is." She waved him to follow her, but he caught her hand and stopped her. The touch undid him—he quickly dropped her hand.

"Gabby, I know where you keep everything. You've taught me how to change her. We'll be fine. Now go."

Her worried eyes met his, and he wanted to hug her and assure her everything—her friend and him watching the baby—would be fine. But he couldn't. Couldn't touch her because holding her would be his downfall.

With her lips in a thin line, she nodded. "Call me for any reason. I don't know how long I'll be gone. She's almost half an hour away."

"I can stay all night."

And with that, she nodded, clutching her purse, and left. At the click of the door, he stared down at Phoebe, asleep in his arms. Her hair was sweaty where her cheek rested against his arm. He caressed her little head and sat back down on the couch.

A few minutes later, Phoebe's eyes blinked open, and spotting his face, she instantly let out a wail.

"Hey there, smiley, you don't need to cry," he said softly. "Your mama's helping a friend. She'll be back a little later."

Her lower lip wobbled, her eyes squeezed shut and her mouth opened wide—letting out the loudest cry he'd ever heard.

He'd never been alone with the baby before. Gabby had always supervised them, and if Phoebe cried, Gabby had known what to do.

How was he supposed to handle this? How could he stop the crying?

"What do you need?" He sprang to his feet. "You hungry? Or do you not like my face?"

He shifted her in his arms, her head at his shoulders, and went into the kitchen. Her cries grew more urgent. His insides were winding tighter and tighter with each wail.

Was Phoebe in pain? What had Gabby told him? His glance fell on the clean bottles lined on the counter.

*Assume she's hungry.* Right. He fiddled with the formula and hoped for the best. Had he prepared the bottle correctly? The wails were pounding into his head—he'd try anything to stop them.

"Here you go, here's your bottle." He tried to give it to her, but she turned her head and cried harder. Her face was brick red, and her little body stiff with tension. "Okay, I take it you're not hungry."

The basket of toys stood in the corner, so he went over and took out a stuffed bunny. "Look at Mr. Bunny." He pretended to make it hop. She paused, her lips wobbling, and then resumed crying.

Once more, he tried to give her the bottle, but by the tone of her cries, he might as well have been lighting her favorite toy on fire.

Why had he thought he could take care of a baby by himself? Gabby would know what was wrong. She'd get her to stop. What if she came back and the baby was still hysterical? She'd never let him take care of his niece again.

*God, I don't know what to do. I hate seeing her upset. How do I make it better?*

He stood up. She still cried and twisted to face away from him. Locking her in his grip, he shifted her to face the television. Her tiny legs dangled as he gently bounced her. Slowly, the cries subsided.

"You didn't want to see my ugly mug, did you?" He kept his voice low. "I don't blame you. But I'd never hurt you. I'm only here because your mama had to leave for a little bit. Her friend needs her—and she's the type of person who will drop everything for her friends."

The phone call he'd ignored from Sam bloomed fresh in his mind. Had Sam been calling for help? If he had taken it, would he have prevented Sam from overdosing a few days later?

He'd been wrapped up in his own misery about Dad selling the company and Robin leaving him—he hadn't wanted to talk to anyone. He'd figured Sam called to tell him about his latest gig or something. He'd never dreamed Sam would die within the week.

Gently kissing the top of Phoebe's head, he tried to push away the guilt. Gabby's confession about her ex earlier had bothered him more than he cared to admit. The fact a guy would use her like that... His muscles tensed, and Phoebe twisted to look back at him. Two fat teardrops clung to her lashes, and her lower lip jutted out.

"Come on, let's get you in your pajamas. You'll feel better." He carried her to her bedroom. Maybe he should have told Gabby the truth—the whole truth—tonight. Sure, he'd given her the condensed version of him and Robin and his dad, but there was more to it. Much more to it.

Why was it still important for him to make her believe he didn't have money? When she so obviously never would expect anything from him?

"She doesn't mind me now, but if she knew everything..." He laid Phoebe on the changing table, grabbed the wipes and put on a fresh diaper. Then he put her pajamas on, snapping them incorrectly twice before redoing it right. She made little babbling noises. She was back to her happy self. "Your mama doesn't like rich guys, especially ones who didn't earn their money.

And I'm not like her. It's midnight and she's helping her friend. I couldn't even answer a call from my brother."

He scooped her up and carried her to the living room.

He didn't deserve a woman like Gabby.

But he wanted to.

Her mind was racing in opposite directions. One thought dominated—help Eden. The other—had she made a ginormous mistake leaving the baby with Dylan?—chased closely behind. Gabby parked her car behind Eden's on the shoulder of the old two-lane road. Turning on her flashlight, she began making her way across the rocky plain, then up the grassy hill to where a clearing was hidden from the road. She knew the spot because Eden had brought her out here on several occasions, including when they'd camped overnight a few months after Mia died. It had been a cathartic experience with millions of twinkling stars in the black sky and just the two of them talking through the grief.

Tonight was equally as clear, and Gabby had no problem seeing the path ahead of her. A dozen worries circled her brain. Would Dylan be able to handle Phoebe? What if something went wrong and he didn't know what to do? Had she warned him about not letting Phoebe have any pillows in her crib? And what if he tried to feed her something she couldn't handle? Did he know what babies could eat? And what about Eden? Why was she hysterical? What had happened?

When she reached the top of the hill, she scanned the flat clearing until she saw Eden sitting on a blanket, her knees bunched up to her chest.

"Hey," Gabby said, jogging to her side. Eden didn't move, so she clumsily folded her legs to a seated position next to her. "What's going on? Why are you out here all alone?"

"I'm always alone, Gabby." Eden continued to stare ahead, her arms wrapped around her knees. "And I'm about to be even more alone."

"What are you talking about?" Gabby's heart leaped to her throat. Eden's tone set her nerves on edge.

She faced her then. "Dad called me after the picnic. He was all excited. Apparently he and Mom bought an RV and plan on traveling the country sooner rather than later."

Gabby cringed. The past four years had been difficult for the entire family.

"I know how close you are to them." Gabby put her arm around Eden's shoulders.

"That's not the worst part. They don't want to ranch anymore. They're going to sell it." She started crying then.

"Oh no." She rubbed Eden's back as she sobbed. "I don't know what to say. It's your home."

She sniffed. "I always thought I'd get married and bring the kids over to the ranch for Christmas and Sunday dinners and…" She hiccuped and cried at the same time. "All of my memories are there. Mia was there. How can they even consider letting some stranger have it all?"

Now she understood why Eden was so upset. This was about Mia as much as it was about losing her home.

"You'll always have your memories of your sister. They're locked up here—" Gabby pointed to her temple "—not in a house."

Eden sniffled and blew her nose into a tissue. "I know

you're right, but it hit me so hard, especially after the picnic."

"What was wrong with the picnic?" She thought about Dylan's observation regarding Eden and Ryder.

"It was so obvious I don't fit in with the guys around here. Judd said two words to me. Cash completely ignored me. And the only guy who made any effort was the one I don't like at all."

"Judd's quiet. The two words he said to you were two more than he said to most of the women there. And you don't want Cash. He's a player." Should she ask about Ryder? "Why don't you like Ryder?"

"I didn't say that," she snapped.

"You weren't talking about Ryder?"

Eden sighed. "It doesn't matter. Let's drop it."

Gabby raised her eyebrows but didn't push it. A shooting star streaked across the sky in front of them. "Did you see that? A shooting star."

"Maybe if I wish on it, my parents won't sell the ranch."

"Maybe." Gabby wanted to give words of comfort, but she couldn't lie to her best friend. "Change can be good sometimes."

"For you." Eden shrugged.

"What do you mean by that?"

"Nothing. I just noticed how Dylan looked at you. He didn't want you out of his sight."

Her heartbeat quickened. Was it true?

"I'm the only one he knows here."

"He wasn't scared, Gabby." Eden blew out a long breath. "He likes you. And I'm glad. I just...well, I want someone to look at me like that. And instead I'm getting kicked out of my house. Maybe Brittany will let me rent the apartment above her studio for a discount."

"It's been a long time since you were on your own. Having your own apartment could be exactly what you need."

"I've never really been on my own. I dormed with three other girls at college, and lived with Mom and Dad during the summers. I like life how it is now."

"Who's to say you won't like it even better a year from now?" Gabby stood and held out a hand to Eden. She took it, stood and Gabby hugged her.

"I can't stand the thought of someone else living in my house, Gabby." Eden turned to head back down the path.

"Understandable."

"I feel like I have no control."

"I know the feeling well." Gabby followed her, shining the flashlight before them.

"Thanks for coming out here. I'm sorry to call so late. I just couldn't process any of this. I felt paralyzed sitting up there, and all I could think to do was call you."

"I'm glad you did. That's what friends are for. You were there for me night and day after Allison died." They reached the bottom of the hill, and Gabby put her hand on Eden's arm to stop her. "You'll always have me. That's one thing that won't change."

"I know. We'll always be friends. I'll get through this. It's not the worst thing in the world. Losing Mia was."

"I wish Mia and Allison were still here."

"Me, too." Eden stared at her with clear eyes. "I think you should get married and have more kids."

"Me?" She forced out a laugh. "I'm not getting married."

"I think you will and sooner than you think." Eden continued walking forward. "You should, you know. Phoebe would get a daddy, and you'd have someone to lean on."

"I don't need anyone to lean on. I have you and the rest of the group."

"It's not the same." Eden headed toward their cars.

She had a point. It wasn't the same, and she knew it. The fact Dylan had been there to watch Phoebe had allowed her to drop everything and come here to help Eden. Without his offer, she would have had to wake someone else, bring the baby or not come at all.

She checked her phone to see if he'd called or texted. Nothing. No news was good news, right?

"Are you going to be okay going home on your own?" Gabby asked as Eden pulled her keys out of her pocket.

"Yeah." Eden hugged her. "Thanks for coming out tonight. I'm sorry to drag you away."

"Don't be sorry. I wanted to come."

"I'll see you tomorrow." Eden got into her car.

"Hey, Eden?"

"Yes?"

"God will get you through this."

Eden nodded. "I hope so, Gabby. I hope so."

Half an hour later, Gabby quietly unlocked her door and tiptoed inside. The television screen glowed, but no sound came from it. Where were Dylan and Phoebe? As stress tightened her lungs, she stepped into the living room. The sight before her drained every ounce of anxiety.

Dylan was sprawled on her couch with Phoebe cuddled up on his chest. Both were sleeping.

It was the most precious sight she could imagine.

Eden's words echoed in her mind. *You should get married and have more kids...sooner than you think.*

At the time, she'd thought it was ridiculous.

Now the idea didn't seem so out there.

"Hey." She tapped the bottom of Dylan's foot. "Wake up. I'm home."

He shifted, curling his arm around Phoebe protectively. *Have mercy.*

"Dylan, wake up." She carefully picked up the baby. Dylan was a heavy sleeper. She carried Phoebe to her room and set her in the crib before returning to the living room.

He'd sat up and was raking his fingers through his hair. She tried not to stare. He looked so sleepy and adorable...and handsome.

"Was she okay for you?" Gabby perched on the edge of the chair.

"What?" He yawned. "Oh, yeah. She was great."

"She didn't cry at all?" Sometimes Gabby got the feeling she was dispensable—that any adult would do in Phoebe's eyes.

"She cried a little after you left." He looked sheepish. "I think she missed you."

"Really?" Her spirits lifted. How messed up was that? She shouldn't be happy the baby cried.

"Yeah, but she settled down." He picked up his shoes and started putting them on. "How is your friend? Everything okay?"

"She'll be fine. She had an unpleasant life surprise."

"I know how that goes." He nodded. "Well, I'll get

out of your hair. Thanks for the picnic and letting me come over—by the way, the Rockies won."

He crossed to the front door. She followed him.

"You don't have to thank me. I should be the one thanking you. Thanks for watching the baby for me—and for offering. It helped me out." It was scary to think she could depend on him. The facts were there, though. He'd come through for her in a jam.

"No problem. I'm glad I could help. See you in church tomorrow?"

"Yes."

He opened the door, hitched his chin to her and left.

She stared at the closed door for several moments.

The whole friend thing had flown out the window the instant she'd spotted him cradling Phoebe on the couch.

She could no longer herd him into the same pasture as Judd and Cash and the other cowboys in town.

Dylan Kingsley made her heart beat faster, and she didn't know how to deal with it.

Erasing the cowboy from her mind was her last hope. If she only knew how...

# Chapter Ten

"Refill your vaccination gun." Friday afternoon, Stu wiped his forehead and pointed to the ancient flatbed truck where coolers and supplies were ready. Dylan nodded and loped over there, grabbed the medicine and refilled it the way Stu had shown him earlier that morning.

The sun was scorching. Several local men and women had joined them for a day of branding and vaccinating. Since his lassoing skills weren't on par with Stu's other regulars, he'd gotten the task of giving the calves their shots. He'd been focused on the task for hours, even though thoughts of Gabby kept trying to distract him. She'd let down her guard Saturday night, and he'd actually come through for her. He'd been reliable, dependable.

It had been easy. He'd been in the right spot at the right time. The thing was, he wanted to be in that same spot for a long, long time.

"What are you waiting for?" One of the men yelled to a teen, shaking Dylan from his thoughts.

The pen where he was standing held calves separated

from their mamas. Dust, loud mooing and thunderous hoofbeats filled the air whenever one of the crew chased down the next calf. Everyone seemed to be enjoying themselves. The calves appeared no worse for wear, either. As soon as each one was done, it trotted off to join its friends like it hadn't been poked with a needle and had a symbol burned into its flesh.

"We have about ten head left, then we can eat." Stu waited with the branding iron in his hand for the next calf to get dragged over.

Dylan prepared to inject another one. At first it had scared him—what if he poked the wrong spot or the calf kicked him?—but he'd quickly gotten the hang of it. In the three weeks he'd been working for Stu, he'd seen two dead calves out in the wild. He wanted to do whatever he could to make sure the rest of them lived.

They finished taking care of the remaining animals, then opened the pen so they could return to their mamas. Everyone packed up quickly and headed over to the old bunkhouse where a few ladies from church had organized a meal to celebrate the day.

Dylan stopped in at his cabin and washed up before joining the rest of the crew. After filling his plate with pulled pork, cheesy potatoes and cookies, he found an empty table and tore into his food. Stu and two elderly women Dylan had seen in church sat with him.

"How are you liking Rendezvous, Dylan?" The white-haired lady in jeans and a patchwork short-sleeved shirt watched him with an expectant air. "I'm Lois Dern, by the way. I've seen you in church with Gabby."

"Good to meet you, Lois." He nodded. "I like it here a lot."

Stu's toothpick bobbed twice.

"I don't believe we've met. I'm Gretchen Sable." Th brown-haired woman he guessed to be in her late sixtie had understanding eyes. "I hear you're Phoebe's uncle.

"Yes, ma'am." He polished off a cookie.

"Gabby is wonderful. A natural with the baby." Loi stared at him as if expecting a reply.

"Um, yes, she is."

"And she's so helpful," Gretchen said. "We think th world of her." Well, that made two of them. He though she was pretty special, too.

"Do you plan on staying in the area long?" Loi asked.

"Um…" He wanted to say yes, but he couldn't. No as things stood at the moment.

"I have to warn you, though, Dylan," Gretchen said in between bites of a potato chip, "Gabby refuses to dat cowboys. If she'd loosen her stance, I'd set her up with my nephew Judd immediately. Have you met Judd?"

Dylan glanced at Stu for help, but he shrugged, lifting his hands as if to say *you're on your own.*

"Yes, I have met him. He's a good guy."

"He is. The best." Gretchen smiled. "So if she won't consider Judd, she probably won't—"

"Nonsense, Gretch." Lois crumpled her napkin "Gabby might not be attracted to Judd."

"Not attracted?" Gretchen's cheeks grew pink. "What are you saying? Judd's ugly? Because I know better."

"Don't twist my words. I'm just saying you've had your heart set on Judd and Gabby together, but neither of them seems all that interested in the other. Admit it."

"Only because she refuses to date cowboys."

"If he liked her, he'd ask her out and keep asking her out until she said yes." Lois picked up her napkin once more and dabbed at her lips.

Gretchen glared at Lois, then turned back to Dylan. "Are you enjoying working on the ranch?"

"I love it. Stu's a great boss." At least he could answer one question truthfully.

"You're a good worker." Stu cocked his head. "You should stay on permanently."

Permanently? His chest swelled. He'd like nothing more than to stay here.

"I appreciate it, Stu," Dylan said. Every day on the ranch was like being at the best summer camp imaginable. Sure, it was hard work, long hours and physically demanding. But it was also peaceful. He could hear himself think when he rode out on Jethro. It drove away the sensation of constantly having to move on.

He had a feeling he'd been trying to find an honest day's work his entire life.

And he'd found it.

Here.

"I'll have to think about it." He met his boss's eyes. Stu nodded.

"Are you going to the Fourth of July parade, Stu?" Gretchen asked.

"I don't know."

"Well, I heard through the grapevine you aren't going to be riding in the parade this year." Lois leaned in. "Understandable with Josiah gone. Why don't you watch the parade with us? We get our chairs set up bright and early to get our spots. I'll tell Frank to set up one for you, too."

"You don't need to go to trouble on my account." St
flicked a glance at Gretchen.

"It's no trouble," Lois said.

"Come with us," Gretchen said. "We know it hasn'
been easy losing your best friend."

"You can come, too." Lois turned to Dylan. "Unles
you planned on sitting with Gabby."

"Uh…" He didn't know what Gabby's plans were
and he hadn't thought about going to the parade. Hadn'
really thought about the Fourth of July Fest at all.

"Well, if you don't, I'm sure Cash McCoy would be
happy to sit with her." Lois leaned back and shrugged
"He'd probably be fine taking her to the festival after
ward, too."

"I'll take her." The words shot out of his mouth. He
did not like the idea of that smarmy Cash guy hang
ing around Gabby and the baby. "That is, if she wants
to go."

"She'll want to go. You know, this town has a lo
to offer." Lois stared at him hard. He squirmed. Why
was he squirming? "Rendezvous is a nice place to set
tle down."

"If only Nolan wasn't buying the inn…" Gretchen
made a tsk-tsk sound.

"He's not for sure buying the inn," Lois said. "But
if he does, my guess is she'll put up with his nonsense
for a while…but not forever."

He'd all but forgotten Gabby was worried about her
job. He let out a small groan. He'd spent Monday and
Wednesday evening with her, and she hadn't mentioned
a thing about Nolan.

"Isn't there anyone else who wants to buy it?" Dylan
watched the ladies. Both of their faces fell.

"Unfortunately, no. And Gabby would never mention it, but we've done the math, and there aren't many opportunities for her here."

Gabby had said something similar a while back. His nerve endings splintered. It wasn't fair of him to keep her in the dark. He needed to do something.

*Yeah, and that something is to tell her the truth and get Phoebe's trust fund and child support set up. Stop being so selfish!*

Selfishness had prevented him from taking Sam's calls. And selfishness was stopping him from doing the right thing now. But what was he supposed to do? He couldn't simply hand Gabby some papers with a *don't worry about money*.

He owed it to her to tell her the truth. He just didn't know if he had the courage to go through with it. Not when his life was finally starting to make sense.

"I might have another buyer!" Babs shuffled the papers on her desk as Gabby sat down after her shift ended on Friday.

"Are you serious?" Gabby's heart leaped to her throat. If someone else bought Mountain View Inn, Nolan couldn't, and she wouldn't have to work for the control freak. "Please tell me you're being serious."

"I'm being serious." Babs's green eyes twinkled under her heavily mascaraed lashes. "It's a silent buyer, or I'd tell you who it is."

"A silent buyer?" Was that good or bad? Did it mean she might be able to keep her job? Her palms grew clammy thinking about it.

"Yes. Dorothy called a few minutes ago to let me know."

"What does it mean? Will they send someone out to see it? Will I get to meet them?"

"Wish I could tell you, sugar, but I don't know." She shrugged. "As soon as I hear something, I'll tell you."

Gabby sank back into her chair. It was good news, yes, but new concerns came to mind. "What if Nolan makes an offer first?"

"He might. If he does, the other buyer could put in a counter offer. My gut tells me if Nolan was in a hurry, the papers would already be signed. You know him. He needs to analyze it to death while he throws his weight around for a while."

Unfortunately, she did know and agreed with the assessment.

"Want me to watch Phoebe so you can go to Fourth of July Fest with your hunk?" Babs scribbled something on a paper.

"What?" She should have prepared herself for this. She knew how Babs's mind worked. "He's not my hunk. And I don't know what I'm doing yet."

"He's a hunk. You can admit it."

Gabby rolled her eyes. Dylan was a hunk—but she didn't need to fan the matchmaking flames Babs enjoyed kindling.

"You know I'm right." Babs pulled a tube of lip gloss out of her purse and ran the wand across her lips. "Anyway, I'd love to take the little butterball off your hands on Saturday. Just let me know."

"Thanks, Babs."

"What are you doing tonight?"

Gabby could feel her neck warm. "Oh, the usual. Pizza."

"You're not telling me something." Babs gave her a shrewd look and pointed the tube at her.

"Dylan is coming over to see the baby."

"So it's a date."

"It's not a date."

"It's a pizza date."

"It's *not* a pizza date."

"Gabrielle." Babs gave her a long, intense stare. She never used her full name. It reminded Gabby of getting scolded. "I had forty-one wonderful years with Herb. We went on adventures together. We bought properties and started businesses. He thought I was the best thing since sliced bread—of course, it helped he was color blind—I don't know many men who could handle my loud style. We were happy. And I miss him more than I ever thought possible."

A lump formed in Gabby's throat. Herb had been a great guy. Babs's bright, over-the-top personality had dimmed in the two years since he'd passed.

"I want you to have the same thing." Her voice softened. "I know you have your whole cowboy rule, but from all accounts, Dylan seems to be a decent guy. At least give him a chance. I want you to find your Herb."

"I want to find my Herb, too, Babs." And she did. "I didn't realize how much until Dylan arrived."

"See?"

"It's not what you think, though." She tried to find the words. "Having him around helping with the baby made me see how nice it could be to have a partner in life. And I would like for Phoebe to have a daddy. But I'm not ready for all that yet."

"Not even with Dylan?"

"Especially not with Dylan." She couldn't go there.

It was too scary. She didn't know him well enough. What if he was laying the groundwork to get her to trust him? And then he showed his true colors? If she allowed herself to care about him, her heart could get smashed into bits. "It would be too complicated, with him being Phoebe's uncle."

"I don't know about that. Just be open to the possibilities, okay, hon?"

"Okay." Her heart had been teetering closer and closer to falling for him, but could she risk it?

"Now, let's get out of here." Babs pushed her chair back. "Did you put Stella on the night shift this weekend?"

"I did. She needs the experience."

"I just hope she doesn't flirt too much. It wouldn't do us a lick of good if she starts batting her eyelashes at a married man."

Gabby laughed. "Don't worry, she uses her flirting energy for good-looking younger guys. I think she has a radar for them or something."

"I'll take your word for it." Babs strolled with her down the hall. "Have fun on your pizza date."

"It's not a—"

Babs laughed. "Sure, it isn't."

"Call me as soon as you hear anything from Dorothy." Gabby waved to her as she exited the building.

"Will do."

Would a silent buyer be like a silent partner? Running the inn from afar? Letting her do her thing? She hoped so. It would be a dream come true.

The only thing better would be to own the inn herself, and that wasn't ever going to happen.

Gabby crossed the rear parking lot to her car. After

unlocking it, she climbed in and stared at the distant mountains for a few moments.

Babs and Herb had been a power couple, and they'd adored each other. Herb had supported Babs's business ventures. He'd been her emotional rock. Gabby had meant it when she'd told Babs she wanted to find her Herb.

She rubbed her chin. The problem was she needed to be in control—of her job, her life and the baby. Any man who wanted to be with her would have to accept her independent nature.

Did a man exist who could handle the full Gabrielle Stover? Dylan seemed to check all the right boxes. But would he try to change her? Or, worse, find someone on the side to fill in the gaps? She turned the key in the ignition. Her heart was already too drawn to him. Anything other than happily-ever-after would crush her. But life was short, and time was moving fast. Should she take a chance or play it safe? She'd have to figure it out soon.

## Chapter Eleven

"I mixed it up this week." Dylan opened the box of pizza in Gabby's kitchen that evening. He'd had a lot to think about since eating with Stu, Lois and Gretchen earlier. After showering, he'd sat on his front porch and pondered his life. And when Gabby came to mind, which she did almost instantly, he'd wondered if he was putting too much importance on money. Why was he assuming she'd be mad when he told her he was rich? "I swapped the sausage for bacon. What do you think?"

"I think my stomach is growling, and it smells exquisite."

Phoebe was strapped into her high chair and happily working on bites of cantaloupe and tiny pieces of soft bread. Her mouth was a gooey mess as she grinned at him. He patted her head. "Hey, smiley, you're enjoying those, aren't you?"

Gabby yawned, covering her mouth to try to hide it, but failing.

"Long day at the office, huh?" He noticed her eyes weren't as animated as usual, and bags had formed under them.

"Not really." She slid a slice of pizza onto her plate.

"Are you nervous about Nolan buying the inn?" He mimicked her movements and joined her at the table with three slices on his plate.

She'd just taken a big bite, and she nodded as cheese stringed between her mouth and the pizza. Holding up her index finger, she finished chewing.

"Yes, I'm still worried, but I did hear some good news today—well, it might be good news."

"What's that?" He ignored his pizza for the moment to take her in. Her hair fell down her back in messy waves. Her hot-pink T-shirt had a scooped neck, revealing a delicate silver necklace with a circle charm.

"Babs might have another buyer."

His muscles involuntarily tightened. "Oh yeah?"

"I can't say anything beyond that, but anyone would be better than Nolan." She quirked her head to the side. "I'm realistic, though. Even if someone else buys it, my job isn't secure."

Dylan bit into the top slice. He'd never had to worry about job security.

"Do you have a backup plan?" he asked.

"Me?" She touched her chest, grinning. "You clearly don't know who you're dealing with. I have backup plans for my backup plan."

Another thing he admired about her.

"The problem is none of them are all that good."

"Let's hear them."

"I could get my insurance license and work for an agency here in town."

He continued eating as he listened.

"The power company sometimes needs people, but the only jobs that come up on a regular basis are maintenance. It would mean being on the road and a lot of physical labor."

He tried to picture her—strong, yes, but with delicate features and a petite frame—out working on power lines. He didn't see her enjoying it.

"The other option is to move somewhere else and manage another hotel."

Move? Somewhere else? He attacked his food a little too forcefully. He liked it in Rendezvous, and she did too. But if she moved, there would be no point in him living here.

Why had he assumed life could—or would—stay as it was?

If Gabby moved, it meant no more playing with Phoebe. No more Friday night pizzas. No more picnics and Rockies games and all the things he was beginning to look forward to. No more racing pulse whenever Gabby was near. No ranching, no community, no life.

"Moving is my last resort." She picked a piece of pepperoni off the plate and popped it in her mouth. The fact moving wasn't at the top of her list reassured him.

"What would be your first resort—you know, if the sky was the limit?"

"Sky's the limit?" A dreamy smile lit her entire face. "I suppose I'd buy the inn myself. Then I wouldn't have to worry about someone coming in and firing me or making my life miserable."

"Would you want the responsibility that comes with it?" From what he could tell, she'd fit into the role well.

"Yes, I would. I love the place. I would renovate the rooms—you know, freshen it up. Make it as inviting as possible. Babs has given me a lot of freedom, so I already know what works and what doesn't."

"You love your job, don't you?"

"I do. I'd hate to give it up for any reason."

What if he made sure she didn't have to give it up? The inn was getting a new owner, whether Nolan bought it or not. Gabby knew the place inside and out. And Dylan had the funds to make it happen.

He wanted to buy it for her.

He glanced at Phoebe smearing her hands on the tray. "You make it look easy, Gabby."

"What?" She blinked rapidly, and the vulnerability in her expression touched him.

"Being a mother and having a successful career."

"Is that a problem?"

"No, not at all." He shook his head. "I admire it about you. I could have used some of your gumption last year."

"When you were traveling?"

"No." He was ready to show her the side of himself that embarrassed him—the self-centered one who'd let down his brother. "After Dad sold the company and my girlfriend dumped me, I pretty much didn't leave my place for two weeks. I was miserable. And, I can admit it now, I was stuck in a pity party of epic proportions. Sam called and I didn't answer."

"I get it. I can throw myself a mean pity party, too."

"But if I would have taken the call…" He lifted his gaze to the ceiling briefly. "I didn't know he had a drug problem. What if he was reaching out for help? What if I had taken the call and said something that would have stopped him from OD'ing?"

Compassion swam in her gray eyes. "It wasn't your fault, Dylan."

He sucked in a breath. He wanted to believe her. "I don't know."

"I do. Some things are in our control and some things aren't. You no more forced Sam to take drugs than I caused the tear in Allison's heart. I hate that they're gone. Hate that we lost them. But it won't do either of us any good to wallow in regrets."

His chest tightened, and a lump formed in his throat as her words sank in and soothed the deepest part of him. He reached across the table and covered her hand with his. "You really think so?"

"I know so." Her eyes shimmered with appreciation. "This world is full of trouble. But Jesus overcame the world—for you and me and Sam and Allison."

It was as if a heavy, rusty weight lifted off his heart. For the first time since Sam's death, he started to believe he wasn't to blame.

His gaze fell to her lips. Why couldn't he look away?

"Do you want to go to the Fourth of July Fest with me?" he blurted out.

"I planned on going…" She lowered her eyelashes. "Babs offered to watch the baby, but you probably want to spend time with Phoebe, too."

"Babs can watch Phoebe."

"You want to be with me? Just me?" Wariness crept into her features.

"Yes." He braced himself for her rejection.

"Like a date?"

"Yeah, a date."

"I don't date cowboys." The words sounded weak.

The smart thing to do would be to distance himself emotionally, but he wasn't ready to slink away and do everything by her rules. Not anymore. He hadn't asserted himself with his father, and he regretted it. He didn't want to make the same mistake with Gabby.

"Could you make an exception?" he asked. "Just this once?"

Silence filled the room. Then she sighed.

"I don't know, Dylan. I don't think it's smart. I mean, you told me you're going to be here a month, and the month is almost over. You haven't mentioned what you're doing after you leave."

She didn't sugarcoat things, that was for sure.

"Stu told me I could stay on permanently." His chest burned as he thought of making Rendezvous permanent. He wanted it. Badly.

"If you stayed, what would you do? Be Stu's ranch hand indefinitely? Do you have goals? Plans? Dreams?"

Goals. Plans. Dreams. His spirits fell. He wasn't enough for her. Dad hadn't thought he was ambitious enough, either. Nor had Robin.

An apology clung to his lips—the assurance that of course he wanted to be more than a ranch hand—but the words refused to come out.

*God, I'm tired of trying to fit into a mold that isn't me.*

He wasn't going to. Not anymore.

"I like being a ranch hand. It suits me." Had he really said those words? "Riding out, checking fence, moving cattle with Stu is exactly what I'm supposed to be doing."

He might as well head to the door now. She'd never accept a mere ranch hand as suitable dating material. If he told her he wanted to own a ranch, maybe then she'd think he was worthy.

"So you're not chasing the dream of owning your own ranch?"

"No." As much as he wanted to impress her, he

wasn't going to. He'd found his authentic self by helping Stu, and he refused to deny it. At this point in his life, owning a ranch would do nothing for him.

"You're not like anyone I've ever met." She framed her chin in the crook between her thumb and index finger. "What if the pay doesn't meet your needs?"

It would be the perfect time to tell her his needs would be met a thousand times over for the rest of his life.

*Tell her the truth. You know you have to.*

A cold sweat broke out on the back of his neck.

He wasn't ready. He needed to prepare—to figure out the right words.

"I don't need much." It was true. But the sinking feeling in his gut proved he shouldn't have taken the easy way out.

Seconds ticked by.

"Okay, I'll go with you to the festival." Her determined chin rose. "Just so we're clear—I will be your date."

He had to be missing something. He'd told her his life goal was to be a ranch hand—a cowboy—and she'd changed her mind about dating him? She'd said yes?

It was his turn to stand. He walked over to her, tipped her chin up and stared into her eyes. Fire, fear and excitement glittered within them.

This woman—he didn't know a woman like her existed. Passionate, selfless, caring, generous. He clenched his jaw.

He loved her.

He was absolutely head over heels in love with this woman.

"I'm going to kiss you." His voice was low as he

watched her reaction. It wouldn't do to scare her off, not when she'd finally opened up enough to let him in.

"I'm not going to stop you." Her words were all bravado, and he could see the previous hurts and questions in her eyes.

He slid his palms up her biceps oh so gently and cupped her face. Slowly, he lowered his lips to hers. He sucked in a breath at the sweetness of them. Then he pressed her closer to him, savoring her supple frame in his arms, the softness of her lips, the rightness of them together.

He'd been waiting for this moment his entire life.

Her arms crept around his neck, and her hand caressed the back of it. The kiss ebbed and flowed, and he wanted to convey how much she meant to him.

Gabby Stover was more than he deserved. She was more than any man deserved.

When he finally broke away, he moved his hands down to her slim waist.

"Well, then..." Her cheeks were flushed, and she looked shell-shocked.

"Yeah." His voice was gravelly. He had so much to say to her and no words to say it.

She smoothed her hair with shaky fingers. "Let's get Phoebe cleaned up and take a walk down at the park. I want to soak in all the summer I can."

He wouldn't argue with that.

Between now and the festival next Saturday, he had to talk to Stu about staying. He also had to tell Gabby the truth about his money. And he'd better call his lawyer to find out the best way forward to purchase the inn.

And somewhere in there he had to tell her more... that he loved her.

Was the timing wrong, though?

He'd gotten Gabby to agree to a date, and he didn't want to scare her off with the L-word. He'd talk to Stu and Ed this week, but Gabby?

He'd wait to confess his net worth and love for her until after the festival. One more week wouldn't hurt a thing.

This changed everything.

Gabby stood on her balcony later that night and touched her fingers to her lips for the thousandth time. Dylan had kissed her! And she'd wanted him to. Because he'd opened up to her about his guilt over Sam. And then, he'd shocked her by explaining his job at Stu's was exactly what he was meant to do. She'd expected him to spin wild dreams about owning a huge cattle ranch and what he'd buy after he'd made it big. Her daddy and Carl had always been chasing fantasies ending in riches.

Dylan wasn't like them.

And if he wasn't like them, there was no reason she shouldn't date him.

He'd been reliable, honest and trustworthy since he'd arrived in Rendezvous.

Babs was right—she could be open to the possibility of a future with Dylan. She certainly thought about him enough. Like all the time—at work, at home—and after that kiss, she doubted she'd get to sleep tonight.

The stars above twinkled, reminding her of last week when she'd met Eden out at the clearing. She'd checked on her a few times, and thankfully, Eden seemed to be back to herself.

Gabby took out her phone and texted her. Dylan kissed me today.

The reply was instant. What?

Yeah, and we're going to the Fourth of July Fest together. As a date.

No way! That's great!

She hesitated before texting what was on her mind.

Do you think I can trust him? What if he ends up being a lying jerk?

A few moments passed before Eden replied. I think you're strong enough to take the chance. If he's a lying jerk, you'll deal with it. If not, you might have found your dream man.

Tears pricked the backs of her eyes.

Thanks, Eden. I needed that.

A smiley emoji appeared.

She set the phone down and enjoyed the light breeze on her face. As much as she'd tried to protect her heart, she'd failed. Big-time. Eden was right. Whatever happened with Dylan, she'd deal with it—good or bad.

She'd already fallen in love with him.

It was hard to admit, but it was impossible to deny.

Chicken and biscuits, she'd fallen in love with a cowboy.

# Chapter Twelve

This had been the best week of his life.

Dylan held Gabby's hand as they strolled past food trucks and dodged children waving American flags. They'd already watched the Fourth of July parade with its line of fire trucks, floats, cowboys and cowgirls riding horseback and the Rendezvous high school marching band cranking out tunes. He was ready to make this town his permanent home.

"Let's get a picture before we eat." He tugged her to stand in front of a banner with the American flag, and they mugged for the camera on his phone before continuing on. "What are you hungry for?"

"Ribs sound good." Gabby pointed to a long line wrapping around a trailer advertising barbecue.

The red, white and blue theme was everywhere. Little flags had been stuck in the ground, patriotic banners were strung across the food trucks and even the picnic tables had red tablecloths.

"What time did you say the baseball game starts?" They'd decided to watch the local team play this afternoon. Later, when it got dark, they were joining the rest of the town to watch the fireworks display. "Do we have time?"

"Plenty of time." She held his hand as they walked. "It doesn't start for another hour."

He'd spent every evening except Tuesday this week with Gabby and Phoebe. They'd talked about their dreams and Phoebe's future. She wanted Phoebe to have a good education, lots of love and faith in the Lord, not in that order. He wanted the same.

He'd been tempted to blurt out the truth a few times, but until he had his plans lined up, he'd remain silent. He hoped Stu would still want to employ him when he told him who he really was. His wealthy background wouldn't matter, would it?

Acid chewed his stomach lining. He'd talked to his lawyer at length. Hopefully, when he told Gabby his real identity, the legal documents Ed had prepared would soften the shock.

Would she be mad? Hate him? She wouldn't hold a little thing like money against him, would she?

He was making mountains out of molehills. It wasn't as if he was a completely different person. So he had money. Lots of it. Big deal. There were worse things he could be—like a murderer or an embezzler.

But his conscience goaded him.

He had to tell her soon.

"Dylan?"

He and Gabby both turned at the high-pitched, feminine voice.

"Dylan Kingsley?" A petite blonde wearing a cowboy hat, sundress and cowboy boots rushed over. He froze. Amanda Bethel. Daughter of real-estate moguls James and Elizabeth Bethel. She'd been a key member in his group of college friends. Her smile lit her face. "It's been forever! How are you? I can't believe I'm bumping into you here."

Should he pretend he didn't know her? Of course not. He wasn't that immature.

"Amanda." He'd be polite, keep it short and nudge her on her way. "Good to see you."

"You, too. Oh, this is my husband, Jack." She twined her hand around the guy's arm. The tall, tanned man looked to be in his early thirties. "Dylan and I went to Texas A&M together. Bree, Charlotte and I used to hang out with him and his frat brothers all the time. We had so much fun. Remember skiing in Aspen over Christmas break sophomore year? And I will never forget the month in Paris and Rome with the crew. Do you ever talk to Travis and Dalton?"

"Uh, no, I don't." Too much information—Amanda was throwing out way too much information. He couldn't even look at Gabby for fear of what he'd see. "When did you get married? Have you been in town long? Did you see the old car show? You don't want to miss it." He pointed in the direction of the park.

"We're newlyweds! And no, we just arrived today. Hey, I'm sorry to hear your dad died." She frowned, then turned to her husband. "Jack, your mother probably worked with him. Kenneth Kingsley."

"Oh, right. King Energy," Jack said, looking bored. "Yes, I remember she did a few projects with your father over the years."

Did they have to spell out everything in his past? This was a disaster. A complete disaster.

"Are you getting in line?" Amanda asked. "We'll join you. Then we can catch up." She flashed her perfect smile toward Gabby. "By the way, I'm Amanda. Are you and Dylan together?"

Gabby stared at the gorgeous woman who'd practically pranced over to them. For once she had no words. Who was this woman with her designer bag and expensive boots? And more importantly, who was the man Gabby had fallen in love with?

The Dylan Kingsley she knew was not the Dylan Kingsley Amanda was greeting.

Had he gone to Texas A&M? Was his father the owner of King Energy, one of the largest energy companies in the country? If he was, why had Dylan let her believe he was just any guy breezing into town?

Had Dylan been lying to her all this time?

Why?

Why would he do that?

"Amanda, this is Gabby Stover. Gabby, Amanda—" He frowned. "You're married now. What is your last name?"

Her laugh tinkled. "Turner. Amanda Turner. We got married last month, and we're working our way to Yellowstone as part of our honeymoon summer."

Gabby dug her fingernails into her palms. Honeymoon summer? Was this woman for real? Who had the money to take an entire summer off for their honeymoon? As the pit in her stomach grew to gaping proportions, Gabby tried to come up with a reasonable explanation for Dylan to be the person Amanda seemed to think he was.

She couldn't think of a single one.

"It was really good to run into you, but we have to go

or we'll be late. We have, ah, plans." Dylan took Gabby's arm and waved to the couple. "Have fun."

She let him lead her away as her head spun. This couldn't be happening—not after such an amazing week. Dylan had stopped by almost every night, and she'd let herself think of them as a couple—a real couple with a future. He'd been terrific with Phoebe, playing with her, changing her, holding her. And Gabby had loved every minute of it. They'd laughed and talked about the future. He'd helped her forget about her job and Allison being gone and Carl's betrayal and her dad's selfish ways.

She'd let herself trust him.

They were almost to the parking lot where Dylan had left his truck. When they reached the tailgate, he finally dropped her hand and stood in front of her. Every muscle in his body seemed to be locked in place, except for his facial muscles—his expression? Pure agony.

And still, she had no words. It might have been the first time in her life she couldn't form a sentence.

Guilt, regret, worry and a shimmer of hope flitted across his face, and it was the last one—the hope—that set her tongue in motion.

"Who was that woman?" She barely recognized her voice it was so calm.

"Amanda and I were in the same friend group in college."

"Texas A&M. I didn't even know you'd gone to college."

A white line rimmed his lips, and his eyes had lost all of their sparkle. "I did. I joined a fraternity, and that was how I met her and her friends—they were in a sorority."

"I see." Her heart started to split open then. "And your dad?"

"Is—was—Kenneth Kingsley, founder and previous owner of King Energy."

"You worked for him."

"I did. I was upper management."

Before her eyes Dylan morphed from traveling cowboy to rich, aimless liar. Rage flickered to life, flaming through her chest.

"The small inheritance wasn't so small." Her words held a bite to them.

"I'm a multimillionaire."

Multimillionaire. A vacuum hollowed out her stomach. She looked back and remembered all his vague replies when they'd met. "So when you said you'd been doing this and that for the past year, you really meant you were bored and traveled because you could."

"I told you I went overseas."

"And you let me believe you were poor."

"You decided that, not me."

"Obviously, you don't need money... Why did you work for Stu? You didn't need a job. You *don't* need a job." Every word she spoke came out harder, sharper, like flint on steel.

"You thought I was a deadbeat."

"You could have explained." Her voice had a strangled quality, kind of like her heart.

"I didn't want to." His jaw tightened.

"Why not?"

"Because I *did* need the job."

She squinted, trying to figure out what he was talking about. "I thought you just said you're a multimillionaire." An out-of-breath sensation had her head spinning.

"It wasn't about the money." He seemed to grow an

inch. "You made it clear I couldn't be around Phoebe unless I had a job."

"Don't give me that." Was he really trying to blame her for his dishonesty? "I didn't want her around a deadbeat. You obviously aren't one."

"I felt like one." His eyes flashed. "Maybe I needed a break from being the son of a mogul."

"And maybe I need a break from my entire life. Do you think I love having to carry on every day as if Allison didn't die? I've supported my sister, my grandma and now my baby—yes, I consider her *my* baby—and I never felt the need to lie to get out of any of it. You lied to me. Even after I told you…" She almost choked on the words. "I told you about my father and Carl. You knew how important honesty is to me, and you stood there and lied to my face."

His face crumpled. "I didn't mean to—"

"Yes, you did." She straightened to her tallest height. "You lied to me on purpose."

His lips drew together in a tight line.

"Why? Why would you do that?" The words flew out. "Why would you look me in the eye and let me believe you were an aimless, traveling cowboy? Was it funny to you? Did you have a good laugh?"

"It wasn't like that."

"Then what was it like? You came into town to meet your niece. Then, for whatever reason, you decide one night isn't enough. You're going to stay. So I told you to get a job." She grimaced as she tried to remember everything. What was she missing? Could anything explain this turn of events? "You could have told me right then, 'Actually, Gabby, I am not a deadbeat and don't need a job,' but you didn't. You went to the ranch." Her voice had risen. "Does Stu know? Does anyone else in town know?" His mouth had dropped open, and she jabbed her finger into his chest. "Am I the last person to know?"

"Know what?" He shook his head, his expression full of pain. "I'm the same guy who showed up a month ago."

"No, you're not." She had to get away from him. "You are not the same guy. Don't kid yourself that you are. You're Dylan Kingsley—spoiled rich kid who can do whatever he wants because of his daddy's money."

And with that, she pivoted to get away.

"Gabby, wait!" He blocked her path, and she shoved his arm to move past him, but he stood his ground. "You're right. I am a spoiled rich kid who can do whatever I want because of my dad's money. I won't argue with you about that."

"Then we're done here."

"No, we're not." He'd been stupid—so stupid—not to have told her all this when he'd arrived. She had every right to hate him, but he couldn't let her walk away. "I should have told you. I wanted to tell you."

"Oh, you *wanted* to tell me. That's great. Let's give the man a round of applause." She pretended to clap. He'd never seen her so angry...and hurt.

"Everything I told you was the truth." He needed to make her see he wasn't an ogre.

"Well, excuse me if I don't care. So your dad sold the company and didn't tell you. Boo-hoo. And your ex only wanted you because of your money. Join the club."

Her words hit him hard. She was right.

He raked his fingers through his hair. "I didn't tell

you because I wanted to make sure you weren't like my mother or my ex. Then, I got to know you, and you were nothing like them. But I didn't know what to say. I didn't know how to tell you. And then... I fell in love with you. I love you, Gabby."

"Liar!" She gave him a final, deadly glare, then broke into a run. He tried to catch her, but she weaved through the crowd, and after several minutes, he dropped his hands to his knees to catch his breath.

He'd never hated himself more.

Letting down Gabby was the worst mistake of his life.

## Chapter Thirteen

"Eden—" Gabby gasped for air "—I have to talk to you."

"What's wrong?" Eden's face wrinkled in concern.

"Everything." She'd sprinted to the park where Eden had told her she was joining Mason, Brittany and Noah for the pet parade. Noah was clapping and pointing to a big dog wearing a red, white and blue handkerchief and star-shaped sunglasses. A chihuahua was right behind him.

"Come on, let's go somewhere we can talk." Eden hooked her arm in Gabby's and told Mason and Brittany she'd see them later.

Gabby's heart raced out of control as she tried to get her breathing back to normal. As they strode out of the park, Eden waved to people they knew until they'd reached her car. Gabby barely registered anything. All she was aware of was the aching pain in her heart.

"My house or yours?" Eden asked.

"Can we go to the ranch? I—I can't be home right now."

"Of course."

The first few miles Gabby stayed silent. She didn't know how to start or what to say. The humiliation of her breakup with Carl roared back. Why hadn't she learned her lesson? She'd tried so hard to steer clear of liars.

She hadn't tried hard enough with Dylan.

She'd reverted to stars-in-her-eyes Gabby—the dumb, gullible girl who knew better than to trust a cowboy. But she'd gone ahead and trusted one anyway.

Eden glanced her way, her forehead wrinkled in concern.

Gabby had to tell her. She might as well blurt it all out now. "Dylan is rich."

"That's great!" Eden's eyes lit up.

"It's not great. It's horrible." How could she explain? She stared out the window, not fully understanding why her pain cut so deep.

"Ok-a-ay. Why is it horrible?"

"It just is. I should never have let down my guard. I wish Dylan Kingsley had never come to Rendezvous. My life was fine until he showed up."

"What aren't you telling me?"

"He's a liar. I hate liars. I…I need to think for a minute." The miles rolled along. Gabby kept replaying the scene near the food truck. Was there something she could have done to have found out the truth sooner? Had she missed clues to Dylan's real identity—or purposely overlooked them to give him the benefit of the doubt?

What else had he lied about?

Eden turned down the gravel drive, and soon she'd parked in front of the house. Gabby got out and followed her to the front door. They made their way in silence to the screened-in porch. Sunshine spilled onto a table containing a ceramic pitcher full of fresh-cut pink roses. The sight unleashed Gabby's emotions.

Her life had been like that flower arrangement—simple, pretty, sweet-smelling—until the day Dylan arrived. And now it was shriveled, sour and ugly.

"He lied to me, Eden." She leaned back as she sat on her favorite couch. "He made me believe he was a drifter with no job or money. And he's really the heir to his father's energy empire. His dad owned King Energy. And Dylan inherited his millions."

"That can't be right." She shook her head. "Why would he take the job at Stu's then?"

"Exactly." She thumped her fist on the throw pillow next to her. "Why would he do that? Was he laughing at me? Pulling a prank on us all?"

"I don't know." Eden bit her lower lip. "He doesn't seem the type."

"What type is he?" She flashed her palms, fingers wide. "I thought I knew him, but I don't. Not at all."

"It doesn't change the fact he's Phoebe's uncle."

"It *does* change the fact I don't want her around him. I am not putting her through the mind games I went through as a kid. And I told him that from day one. She is too precious for me to let some lying jerk mess with her emotions."

"You don't have to get it all figured out today," she said quietly. "You're mad. When you cool down, you'll know what to do."

"I know what to do." Gabby nodded swiftly. "I'm done with him and so is Phoebe."

"Is that fair to her?" Eden sighed. "Why don't you tell me what happened?"

She took a deep breath. Maybe Eden could help her

connect the dots. It seemed like there was a giant piece of the puzzle missing, and as much as she tried to convince herself the piece was Dylan as the bad guy, something wasn't adding up.

"We were getting in line for ribs, and this perky blonde bounced over..." She told Eden everything—the college tales, the honeymoon summer and the argument by Dylan's car. "He claimed he got the job because I forced him to so he could be around Phoebe and that he's the same guy he was. Then he threw out 'I love you,' like it was supposed to make everything all right."

She still huffed over the last part. How dare he? How dare he pretend to love her to get his way?

"He told you he loves you?" Eden's eyes grew round. "What did you say?"

"I called him a liar and sprinted to the park to find you."

"Oh." She studied her nails. "Have you considered he might actually love you?"

"No, I haven't," she snapped. "Carl told me he loved me, too. And guess what? He was married. Married! To another woman. Using me, taking my money—so, no, I don't believe a liar who tells me he loves me."

"Married? Oh, Gabby. I had no idea. No wonder you hate cowboys." Eden pressed her hand to her chest. "I'm sorry."

"Yeah, well, so am I." Her anger ebbed and a knot formed in her throat. She'd never told anyone about Carl being married, and the embarrassment of it hit her fresh. "I never should have trusted Dylan. I knew better."

Eden stood. "Why don't I get us some iced tea?"

Gabby nodded, trying to will away the tears forming, but one dropped, then another. She swiped them away.

She'd been such a dummy. Hadn't she told herself not to trust him? That all cowboys were liars? But no, she'd opened her heart…and the worst part was?

She was in love with him.

She loved another lying loser.

Eden returned and handed her a glass.

"I have the worst taste in men."

"You couldn't have known Dylan would lie to you."

"Yes, I could." She took a sip, letting the ice-cold tea soothe her aching throat. "I knew. I knew the minute he walked into the inn that he was trouble. I blame myself."

Eden thought about it a minute. "You're assuming he's like Carl, though. That's not fair. Being rich and being married are two different things."

"Being a scumbag liar is the same thing."

"I've met Dylan, and he is not a scumbag. He seems genuine."

"It's an act." But was it?

"I don't think so, Gabby. I think he really likes you. You told me yourself he's wonderful with Phoebe. Reliable. Always shows up when he says he will."

She could feel her anger weakening. He had been dependable and reliable. But maybe it was all an act. "It really doesn't matter. He lied to me, and I'm done."

"No one is perfect." Eden's lips lifted in a brief, sad smile. "I'm not saying you're wrong. Maybe he is a terrible person. Maybe he's not. But given everything you've told me—he really might love you. And I know you have feelings for him. Shouldn't you at least consider giving him some grace?"

Grace.

What a loaded word.

Grace meant forgiving. And forgiving meant lyin
down and being a doormat—*Here, walk all over me!*

"I don't think so, Eden." She shook her head.

Eden nodded in understanding, but the strain aroun
her mouth revealed her disappointment. "Pray about i
And I'll pray for you, too."

The last thing she wanted to do was pray. She wante
to crawl into her bed and never come out again.

He never should have stayed in Rendezvous. Tha
night Dylan paced the length of his porch. Back an
forth. Back and forth.

His heart was wrapped in barbed wire and gettin,
squeezed tighter by the minute. He'd lost Gabby's trus
and he hadn't realized how important it was until she'
called him a liar.

He was a liar. A fraud.

And tomorrow, when he told Stu the truth—that he'
misled him, had zero ranching experience and didn'
need the job or the money—he'd see the same disap
pointment and loathing from him that he had from
Gabby.

Maybe he should sneak out of town tonight. Then h
wouldn't have to confess to Stu or worry about bump
ing into Gabby again.

He paused, set his hand on the porch rail and gazed
unseeing out at the stars. Pops from the fireworks in th
distance filled the air. He should have been watchin
them with Gabby. If Amanda hadn't arrived and ru
ined everything, he'd be sitting there with Gabby now
Holding her hand. Planning how to tell her he wasn'
the drifter she'd assumed.

He smacked the rail. It wouldn't have mattered. Ei

her way, he'd lied, and Gabby would hate him—did hate him. He didn't blame her. He hated himself.

Covering his face with his hands, he wiped his cheeks. How would this affect Phoebe? Would Gabby keep her from him? He couldn't bear not to see the baby's smiling face anymore.

Man, he'd blown it.

The humid air made his skin sticky, but he stayed outside.

What was he going to do now?

He thought of the documents his lawyer had drafted and emailed on Thursday. Dylan had the trust fund ready. He didn't have the child support documents drawn up, though—he'd foolishly believed they wouldn't be necessary. But a future with Gabby wasn't going to happen.

Still, the purchase agreement for the inn would ensure she had the freedom she wanted. He could feel good about that, he supposed.

Maybe the people closest to him were better off without him in their life.

He thought back to the night Sam died. How the paramedics found his little brother on the floor of some guy's apartment. He'd been dead for a few hours. He'd died alone in a stranger's house. His sensitive, caring, brilliant brother—gone. Just like that.

Dylan squeezed his eyes shut. Gabby was right—there was nothing he could have done to prevent his death.

The helplessness of it all crushed him.

He swallowed the lump in his throat. But there was something he could have done to prevent Gabby from hating him. Why hadn't he told her the truth? From the minute he'd met her, he'd been fascinated by her. She challenged him, pushed him and ultimately accepte him. He loved her more than he'd ever loved anyone.

Why had he been so stupid?

It had taken him less than two days to figure ou Gabby was nothing like his mom or Robin. He shoul have told her he was rich then.

But he hadn't trusted her. Hadn't really trusted him self.

Did he now?

He peered at the outlines of the ranch before him. H hadn't just fallen in love with Gabby and Phoebe. He' fallen in love with the cowboy life. This ranch. Help ing Stu with the cattle, fishing, being one of the guys

In some ways Stu was the dad he'd always wanted

And he'd deceived him, too.

Tomorrow was going to be one of the toughest day of his life, but if he'd learned anything in Rendezvou: he'd learned he was strong enough to handle it.

Was he strong enough, though, to say goodbye to th first real home he'd had in years? To a job he was pas sionate about? To the woman he loved?

He went inside and closed the door.

It was going to be a long, sleepless night.

He'd do the right thing tomorrow. And after that? A long, empty future awaited him.

## Chapter Fourteen

She had a raging headache, a million questions and zero answers. Gabby padded into Phoebe's room a little after two in the morning. So much of her life had turned upside down in the past month. The only thing she knew for sure was she would do anything to protect and love her precious baby, and not just for Allison's sake—for her own.

*No one is perfect.* As much as she tried to drown out Eden's words from earlier, they kept repeating in her head.

What Dylan had done went beyond not perfect, though. Didn't Eden get it? And her whole grace suggestion—Gabby shook her head. No way. He didn't deserve it.

She kissed her index finger and gently touched Phoebe's forehead with it before heading to the living room. After dragging a soft blanket out of the closet, she settled on the couch, draping it across her legs.

Some offenses were too big to forgive.

Hiking the blanket to her chin, she recounted why

she'd been right to cut ties with her dad and with Carl And now with Dylan.

They'd put their own selfish needs above hers. She'd never asked for much. She hadn't held it against her dad when she and Allison had gone hungry and woke up during the winter months to see their own breath She hadn't minded helping Carl out financially because she'd loved him. She'd loved both Dad and Carl, and she'd believed they'd loved her, too.

And Dylan… She'd opened up to him, shared the baby with him, introduced him to her friends…

He'd abused her trust.

The same as her father. The same as Carl.

*What he did wasn't as bad as Daddy or Carl.*

Where had that thought come from? Of course, i was as bad.

*I judged him the day he came to Rendezvous. I'm judging him now.*

It hadn't been judging… It had been forming an impression. And she had every right to judge him now.

She would never do to him what he'd done to her She wouldn't have lied to him about anything. She was honest.

*No one is perfect.*

The secret shame she'd pushed deep inside threatened to burst out of her. She might not have lied to Dylan, but she'd been lying to herself for years.

Why couldn't she get real with herself about Carl? The signs had been there and she'd ignored them. Finding out he was married wasn't as big a shock as she pretended it was.

Her lungs tightened as if she'd been punched.

*I demand the truth, but if I value it so much, I need to be honest with myself.*

She swung her legs over the couch then buried her face in her hands. It was true—she'd suspected Carl was married but hadn't wanted to believe it. The clues had been there—the odd hours they'd meet and his reluctance to spend time together out in public. One time she'd actually caught him taking off his ring and slipping it inside his pocket, and she'd never said a word.

*I'm not perfect. Eden's right. No one is.*

All the Tuesdays for the past couple of years with her friends came to mind. They prayed for each other and read from the Bible and supported each other. And it made her feel so virtuous. But she was a hypocrite. The biggest hypocrite imaginable.

She wasn't perfect. Never had been. Never would be.

*Lord, forgive me for expecting perfection and not extending grace. I'm not perfect, and yet, You give me grace all the time.*

It was time for her to forgive her father and Carl.

*Lord, I forgive Carl. I don't like him or ever want to see him again, but I forgive him. And I forgive my dad. Please give me peace about them.*

It hit her that forgiveness didn't always mean reconciliation, nor did it make her a doormat.

Maybe the real reason she didn't want to forgive Dylan was out of fear.

If she forgave him, allowed him back into her heart, he might hurt her again. She might wake up in a few months and realize she'd been right all along that he'd never cared about her the way she did him.

But if she didn't forgive…would she expect every

man who came into her life to live up to a set of stan
dards no one could reach?

The ticktock of the clock kept her company as she
struggled with how to move forward.

He'd said he was the same guy who'd arrived a month
ago, but could she believe him?

She didn't know.

Every man she'd let into the most special place in
her heart had let her down. And now that she'd fallen
for Dylan, she couldn't get the image of them together
out of her mind. For years she'd wanted it all but had
refused to admit it. She wanted a loving husband, a
family of her own.

Gabby rubbed her temple. She didn't even know what
a loving husband looked like.

She'd thought he looked like Dylan, but now? She
had no clue.

"I need to talk to you." Dylan held his cowboy hat
between his hands as he stood on Stu's porch the next
morning. The sun was still low on the horizon, but he
knew Stu would be up. Dylan hadn't gotten any sleep,
and his stubble made his face as scratchy as his heart.

"What's going on? Something wrong with the
horses? The cattle?" Stu shoved his stockinged feet
into cowboy boots.

"No, nothing's wrong with the ranch." He sighed.
"It's me."

Somehow Stu had managed to insert his toothpick
between his teeth. He nodded, the toothpick moving up
and down. "We'll talk better riding."

They strode in silence across the yard to the stables and tack room, and it didn't take long to saddle

up and head down the trail toward the creek. The heat was already rising as they navigated familiar gullies and climbed hills. Dylan's nerves ratcheted the farther they went. At what point would Stu stop? And how was Dylan going to explain? He'd figured he'd tell Stu everything on his porch, sprint back to his cabin, load the truck, stop at Gabby's and…disappear.

"You see that clearing up ahead?" Stu pointed to a clump of trees with sunlight shining through them. "We'll stop there."

Soon they'd dismounted and were tying off the horses. Dylan marveled at the beautiful vista. They stood on a grassy hill with a panoramic view of the mountains. Smaller ridges lined the ground between them and the mountain range.

"Wow." He took it all in for a minute.

"This is where Josiah and I used to come every September. We'd talk about the ranch. What worked that year and what we'd do differently the next."

Now he felt even worse. He was going to ruin a special spot for Stu.

"Maybe we should ride somewhere else." He looked back at the horses.

"Nah. This is a good talking place. Have a seat." Stu gestured to a few stumps, and Dylan sat on one. His boss took the other. "What's on your mind?"

He didn't know where to begin. All night he'd tossed and turned, going over the same mistakes again and again. Maybe he'd be best off admitting he was rich right off the bat.

"I haven't been honest with you." Dylan stared down at his dirty cowboy boots, then met Stu's eyes. "I came here under false pretenses. I've never ranched. I don't need the money. I don't even need this job."

The toothpick bobbed slowly.

"I'm rich." He made the word sound like he'd told him he was a serial killer. "My dad owned King Energy. I used to work for him, but he sold the company. He didn't want me running it. Then he died about a month later. I inherited everything."

The toothpick paused. Was that a twinkle in Stu's eyes?

He pressed on. "My stepbrother died of a drug overdose a few weeks after Dad sold the company. And I didn't even take his call the week he died."

Why wasn't Stu saying anything?

He didn't know what else to say, so he sat there.

"Is that everything?" Stu asked.

He almost said yes, but it would be a lie, and Gabby hated liars—and he didn't want to be that guy anymore. "No, there's more. I love this job, and I'm in love with Gabby Stover. I lied to her, too. She hates me. I don't blame her."

"What'd you lie to her about?"

"The same as I did you. She thought I was some deadbeat cowboy for hire. She was the one who told me to work here, so I did."

"Why'd you do that?"

"I—" He raised his face to the sky. It was going to sound so stupid. But he owed Stu the truth. "I always wanted to be a cowboy."

Stu's face gave away nothing. "Was it the only reason?"

"No." He hung his head. "I'd spent the past year traveling around the world. And I had no purpose. No place to belong. I guess I wanted to see if I could belong here."

"And did you?"

"Yeah." Closing his eyes, he inhaled the fresh Wyoming air. Not a sound could be heard except birds singing in the trees and the gentle breeze against the leaves. "I did. I do. I belong here."

"So what's the problem?"

"What do you mean? I lied to you. I lied to her. I've got to go."

"Says who?"

"Says…" He hesitated. It wouldn't be fair to stay here if Gabby hated him. He wouldn't make her life miserable. "Me."

"Bah." He waved him off. "I don't care about any of that."

He didn't?

"I knew you weren't familiar with ranching, but you showed up at the right time. You're a hard worker, dependable, and you've got the heart for it. I've been struggling since Josiah died—even his horse, Jethro, was struggling—until you came along. You've given me a spring in my step to keep this place going."

The words wriggled into his heart, coated the raw spots with healing balm.

"I don't know what went on with your daddy, but it seems to me he missed out on a fine young man. As for your brother and the drugs, well, you can't compete with them. He was addicted, son. Nothing you could have done. Let it go."

A sudden burst of emotion pressed tears against his eyes.

Stu kicked at the ground. "I've hired a lot of cowboys

over the years, and they weren't all living the right way. I tried to clean them up, too, and…" He turned away. "I couldn't. It takes time and prayer to realize there's only so much you can do when someone is fighting an addiction. It's their battle. Not yours."

Dylan clenched his jaw to keep his emotions under wraps.

"Listen," Stu said. "I've known Gabby Stover for years. She's a quality gal. A fine woman. And she's never met a cowboy she liked…until you came along. I don't know what all you two've got going, but if it's a matter of you not telling her you've got money, well, I think you'll be able to work it out."

Dylan wanted to believe it, but… "I don't think so. Honesty is very important to her."

"Well, then, I guess we'd better pray about it, huh? Cuz I want you to stay on as my right-hand man. Yes, you'll get a raise. No, you will not turn down the pay. You earn your money around here."

Wait. Stu wasn't disappointed in him? He was promoting him?

"I don't know what to say," Dylan said, shaking his head in wonder.

"Say yes."

He wanted to—oh, how he wanted to. "I have to talk to Gabby. I appreciate the offer, but I can't accept it unless…well, I probably won't be able to accept it." Stu had a forgiving nature, but he doubted Gabby had cooled down or would ever see him through compassionate eyes again.

"We'll see about that. Now, head back and get cleaned up. You want to look your best when you talk to her."

Stu didn't get it—Gabby wasn't just any girl. She'd let him into her life and allowed him to spend time with the baby. She'd trusted him. And he'd let her down.

They mounted the horses once more and headed back.

The urge to pray hit him hard.

*Thank You, God, for Stu's friendship. He may be the first person who's ever accepted me for who I am. Well, that's not true. Gabby did, too. And that's why I love her.*

He didn't deserve Stu, either, but the man had brushed away his dishonesty as if it was nothing.

The same way God did.

*You're the One who's always accepted me, haven't You? How did I not see it?*

With each passing moment, his heart expanded. The realization hit him—whether he was worthy of Gabby or not, he finally felt worthy of himself.

He was finally comfortable in his own skin.

He was Dylan Kingsley, and he didn't need to define himself by his father, his money or his past.

He'd found himself in Rendezvous. He'd found home.

After three hours of sleep, two cups of coffee and a full hour of ruminating, Gabby was ready to think logically about Dylan.

She'd already gathered all of the details about his life that he'd shared with her, including Sam's death, his father's selling the family company, his traveling around the world, his mom using him as a pawn after the divorce and how his ex manipulated him for money, too.

She didn't think he'd lied about any of it.

The facts appeared in a different light when she'd

thought he was an everyday Joe as opposed to a multimillionaire.

The only thing he'd really hidden from her—that she knew of—was the fact he was rich. And even she could concede he'd had good reasons for it.

Given what little she knew of his childhood and his ex, it made sense for him to not advertise he was wealthy.

She took a long drink of coffee number three. Plus there was her own attitude. She cringed thinking of how she'd labeled Nolan as a rich kid who'd be nothing without his daddy's money. And then she'd slapped the same label on Dylan yesterday afternoon.

Not her finest moment.

Which left her...where? How was she supposed to move forward?

She still loved him. But she couldn't trust him. And deep down, she didn't believe he loved her. Why would he? They'd known each other for a month, spent time playing with the baby and gone on one date. Guys like him wouldn't fall in love that quickly, and especially not with her.

Tracing the rim of her mug, she sighed. Maybe that was the real problem. She still didn't believe a guy could love her.

If she was wrong about Dylan—if he *did* love her— what would she be throwing away?

Like a movie montage, she pictured him standing in her doorway with a pizza, then trying to diaper Phoebe for the first time, laughing at her tales from the inn, grinning as he explained how to vaccinate a calf. And then she saw him kissing her, how right it had felt to be in his arms, how good it had felt to be wanted, needed.

His kiss hadn't demanded—it had asked, it had given—just like Dylan himself.

Had he ever demanded anything from her?

She tapped the side of her mug. He'd accepted her conditions from day one. He'd followed her schedule, gotten a job on Stu's ranch, been there when she needed him. He'd spent the last year traveling alone. He'd lost both his dad and brother. He'd also lost his job—his place in the world.

Suddenly, his money seemed like the least important thing about him.

Her heart climbed to her throat. She'd been wrong about him. So wrong.

He really was the same guy who'd shown up last month.

Why else would he work long hours on a ranch and live in a tiny cabin with no air-conditioning? Yes, it was to be near Phoebe, but that couldn't be the only reason. He loved her—had to love her.

Was he still in town? Or had she driven him away?

Glancing down at her attire, she shuddered. Shower first. Call him later.

It was time to give him the benefit of the doubt.

It was time to take a chance—a real chance—on love.

## Chapter Fifteen

$\textasciitilde$

Dylan took a deep breath and went through his mental checklist. Bouquet of peonies from Gretchen Sable's flower garden. Check. Folder with legal documents. Check. Humble attitude. Check. Tell Gabby she was everything to him and he didn't want to live without her or Phoebe. Almost check.

After returning to his cabin earlier, he'd promptly showered and put on his Sunday best. Stu had taken it upon himself to call Gretchen to ask for the flowers, then texted Dylan that Gretchen would have them ready after church. Dylan had prayed for strength during the early service then picked up the flowers on his way to Gabby's place. He just hoped she would answer the door and hear him out.

He had so much to say.

With two sharp knocks, he stood his ground, clenching and unclenching his jaw as he strained to hear footsteps. He was preparing to knock again when the door opened. Gabby held Phoebe on her hip, and her eyes widened as she took him in.

"Can I come in?" He fully expected her to slam the

door in his face. She didn't say a word, simply moved to the side so he could enter. She wore a pretty sundress, and her hair flowed over her shoulders. His heart skipped a beat at how beautiful and vulnerable she looked. "These are for you."

She took them and set the paper-wrapped bouquet on the table.

This wasn't boding well. At least she'd let him inside. He held his finger out, and Phoebe wrapped her tiny hand around it, grinning and bouncing. "Hey, smiley."

Gabby still hadn't spoken, so he stood there awkwardly for a moment.

"Can we sit down?" he asked.

"Sure." They went to the living room. Gabby put Phoebe on her play mat, then sat on the chair with one leg crossed over the other, while he set his folder next to him and perched on the edge of the couch.

"First, I apologize for not being honest with you. I misled you about my financial situation." Her face became a plaster mask. He couldn't detect a single emotion. "And, yes, my dad owned King Energy and I worked for him. Everything else I told you was true. Sam died soon after Dad sold the company. I'd stupidly thought Dad and I would grow close and he'd make me his partner. Instead, he sold it and I found out from his administrative assistant. He died two weeks later. A week after that, my ex-girlfriend—who dumped me because in her words I was 'going nowhere'—came back into my life all sympathy and smiles. It was at that point I took off. Flew to Europe."

The expression in her eyes softened.

He continued. "You told me you didn't want Phoebe around a deadbeat—and you were right. I was a deadbeat when I showed up here. I hadn't had a job in over a year, and my position before then was a glorified token job given to me by my dad. I might as well have been a drifting cowboy looking for work—I had no purpose, no reason to live, really."

She shifted in her seat.

"So when I came here and saw Sam's eyes in the cutest baby I'd ever seen, something in me sprang to life. And the fact you weren't taking any nonsense anchored me. You even mistook me for a cowboy. As a teen, the only thing I aspired to be was a cowboy—I admired the tough, hardworking men I'd watched on my friend's ranch. And I thought, yeah, I don't have to travel anymore. I could be a cowboy for a while."

He rubbed his hand across his mouth. It was time to tell her the scary stuff. *God, give me courage.*

"Stu took a chance on me. Working with him makes me feel alive—and he's been patient with me, teaching me things my father didn't. And you—you took a chance on me. You let me spend time with you and Phoebe. Showed me how to take care of her. Introduced me to your friends. Made me feel like I could belong here."

Tears glistened in her eyes, and he wasn't sure if it was a good sign or a bad one.

"I knew I had to tell you the truth, but I was so afraid you'd reject me. This is the first place that's felt like home for me. I have a purpose here. Because of you." He reached for the file and opened it. He took out the first set of documents and handed them to her. She refused them, so he set them on the end table near her. "I always intended on providing for Sam's child. I've set up a trust fund for Phoebe. That's the paperwork for it."

Gabby stared unseeing up at the corner of the ceiling. A tear dropped on her cheek.

"I can see you're upset. I don't blame you. If I could do it over, I would have told you the truth the day after I arrived. It was unforgivable. You're right—I know how much you value honesty. And it may be late, but I'm being as real as I can possibly be right now. You gave me hope. You helped me find myself. And I love you. I love you so much. I will never stop loving you."

He pulled out the other sheaf of papers in his file.

"That's why I want you to have this." He handed her the papers. "You've given and given and given your entire life. Maybe it's time someone gave you something for a change."

Her lips were drawn together, and she still didn't speak. But she took the papers from him. She scanned the top sheet, her face paling.

He braced himself. Would she accept his gift?

"You can't be serious." Her voice held a spark of anger.

"I'm serious."

"You bought me Mountain View Inn?" She didn't sound happy.

"I did."

"It's bad enough you lied to me, but now you think you can buy my affection?" She threw the packet at him. The staple kept the papers from scattering. "I don't want your money. I don't want your inn."

Didn't he understand her at all? Gabby's heart couldn't take any more of this. Every word he'd said had pierced her in the most vulnerable places. His sincerity and the picture he'd painted of his life before Rendezvous had made her want to wrap him in her arms and never let him go. His money hadn't made him entitled. It had made him lonely, isolated and purposeless.

And then he had to go and buy her the inn.

"You can *never* buy my love." She sprang to her feet and crossed her arms over her chest. "I don't know how they do it down in Texas or in the circles you run in, but around here you don't give someone an expensive gift and think she'll fall into your arms."

"That's not what this is about." He stood, too, running his fingers through his hair.

"You know, I was ready to forgive you. And my heart hurts for you, for your life before you arrived. But I don't think I can forgive this." She waved her hand toward the packet of papers, which had landed on the couch.

"I'm not trying to buy your love. It never crossed my mind. I had my lawyer contact the listing agent last week. You deserve to own the inn. You don't need to worry about Nolan or anyone else coming in and making your life miserable. I don't want you to fear losing your job. You've been running the place for years. You have a vision for it. The only thing you don't have is the money to buy it. And it's the only thing I had to give you."

"It's not the only thing you can give me, Dylan." She lifted her chin. "It isn't even the best thing. You don't get it, do you?"

"Get what?" His eyes pleaded with her.

"Your money is the least attractive thing about you." She stared at him. Why did he have to say such nice things? Why did he have to be so generous? She couldn't hate him, no matter how much she wanted to. A sense of peace filled her body from her head to her toes.

She was ready to take a chance on him.

"You're humble. Undemanding. Generous. Kind. The thing I admire most about you is your lack of ego. You're living in a tiny cabin without air-conditioning, working as a ranch hand, being considerate of my schedule, helping with the baby. You've shown me what real love—a partner—looks like."

His shoulders drew back, and his mouth dropped open.

"I don't like that you lied to me—"

"It was unforgivable." His chin dropped to his chest.

"No, Dylan, it wasn't." She took a step closer to him. "Nothing is unforgivable. And nothing should be. I forgive you."

He met her eyes, and his gleamed with wonder.

"As for those ridiculous papers—" she pursed her lips, shook her head and brought her fist to her mouth "—I don't even know what to say. So I guess it's time for me to be honest with you."

He inhaled and held it.

"I judged you from the minute I met you. Decided you were just like my daddy and my ex-boyfriend. Everything you did I saw through eyes colored by my past. And that wasn't fair to you. You confessed very private, personal things to me, and I'm going to do the same. Carl, my ex-boyfriend, didn't just use me for money. He also lied to me in the most terrible way. He was married, and I didn't know it. But as time wore on, I noticed signs. I suspected he had a wife, and I was so smitten, I pretended I hadn't."

"Gabby—"

"No, let me finish." She held her arm out. "Letting you into my life was hard not only because I didn't trust you, but because I didn't trust myself. You were patient with me. And I slowly began to think…"

He looked like he was going to speak. But she couldn't let him, not yet, not when she still had the most important thing to say.

"Dylan—" her throat grew so tight she almost choked "—I love you. I'm scared. I'm terrified you're going to break my heart."

Wonder filled his eyes. In two steps he was directly in front of her, his arms wrapped around her back, and she sank into his embrace.

"Do you mean it? Do you really love me?" He leaned back to stare into her eyes.

She nodded, tears threatening to fall again.

"I'll never break your heart. It's the most precious gift I've ever been given. I'll do anything to earn your trust."

"It's hard for me," she admitted. "Do you think you have the patience to take it slow?"

"I have forever, Gabby." His grin spread across his face. "I love you. Nothing could change that."

When his lips pressed against hers, she knew taking a chance on him would be the best decision she ever made. A thrill rushed through her body. She'd found a man who valued her. She wanted those arms around her for the rest of her life.

He broke away and stroked her hair. "What do you want me to do about the inn? Shred the purchase agreement? I didn't buy it to win your love. I hope you know that."

For the first time it hit her. He truly had bought Mountain View Inn for her—not as a bribe, but as a gift.

"You really bought me the inn?" She couldn't wrap her brain around it.

He nodded. "No strings attached."

"There are always strings somewhere..." She narrowed her eyes.

"Not this time." His hands slid down to her waist. "Go ahead and read the purchase agreement if you don't believe me. It's in your name. My name is nowhere on it—I was the money behind it, nothing more."

He shifted toward the couch to get the papers, but she tugged him back to her. "I'll take your word for it, cowboy. Why don't you kiss me again?"

His lips curved into a wicked grin. "Anything you want. Just say you'll be mine."

"I'm yours."

As he lowered his mouth to hers, a loud "ba-ba-ba" interrupted them. Phoebe had pulled herself up and was standing next to the couch, holding on to it and bouncing.

Dylan met Gabby's eyes and laughed. "Someone's happy."

"That makes two of us." She stepped back. "What happens now? Does everything change?"

"Nothing's changing." He shook his head. "Stu wants me to stay on as his right-hand man. I'm getting a raise."

His face was so bright with joy, she couldn't help but laugh. "A raise, huh?"

"Yeah, it feels good to earn an honest day's wage."

She couldn't argue with that.

"I have a lot to learn—about ranching, raising a baby, Wyoming…" He tugged her close to him again.

"I'll be happy to help fill you in." She wound her arms around his neck.

"I need a lot of help." He dropped a kiss on her lips.

"Well, I'm good with the baby and Wyoming thing. But ranching? You're on your own."

His grin spread from ear to ear. "Thanks, Gabby."

"For what?"

"For giving me a place to belong. For giving me a purpose."

"You have it all wrong." She pressed her finger in the cleft of his chin. "You gave me a place to belong. In your arms. Thank you for buying me the inn. I…I can't believe you did it. No one has ever been so extravagant."

"Is it too much? I can sell it…"

"Don't you dare, Dylan Kingsley." She playfully slapped his chest. "I want it. Thank you. I don't know how I'll ever thank you enough."

"Why don't you start with a kiss?"

"Done."

# Epilogue

"You can't trust just any cowboy." Gabby didn't look up from her computer at the front counter of Mountain View Inn. The late October sun streamed through the windows, landing on the new hardwood floors that had been laid as part of the hotel renovation. "You've got to make sure they have character—values."

"I'd give the one outside a shot if he had eyes for any girl other than you." Stella scanned the printout of the housekeeping checklist. She'd gotten more dependable in the past four months. There was hope for her yet.

"I wouldn't blame you." Gabby smiled at her.

Dylan walked inside carrying a bouquet of two dozen red roses. He wore dark jeans, cowboy boots and a button-down shirt open at the collar. His Stetson completed the picture of quintessential cowboy. She inwardly swooned. The man filled her heart.

"I'm looking for Gabrielle Stover." His brown eyes twinkled.

"You're looking at her." She bit her lower lip in anticipation. What was he doing? This wasn't the first time he'd brought her flowers, but something was different about him.

"Come with me." He held out his hand, and she exchanged a curious glance with Stella, who shrugged, before rounding the counter and taking his hand.

He led her to the lobby and stopped in front of the floor-to-ceiling stone fireplace complete with a crackling fire. He faced her then, standing inches from her.

"These are for you." He handed her the flowers. She inhaled their lovely scent.

"Thank you."

Then, keeping her hand in his, he lowered himself to one knee. Her heart began hammering so quickly, she thought it might explode. He was proposing!

"Gabrielle Stover, four months ago, I walked into this very inn, and my life changed forever. I found my niece. I found my calling. And I found myself. I couldn't have found any of it without you. You're the reason I wake up smiling. You're the reason I fall asleep anticipating another day. You're my everything. I want to spend forever with you. Will you marry me?"

He held a small, square box in his hand. He opened it, revealing an intricate diamond ring.

She blinked away the tears. "Yes, oh yes!"

He slid the ring on her finger, and she threw her arms around his neck and kissed him. He rose, not breaking their kiss. Then he tightened his grip and deepened the kiss. And she was lost. Lost in the safety of his arms and heart.

A round of applause interrupted them, and they both turned. The lobby had filled with friends and guests. Eden ran to her and hugged her, her eyes misting up.

"What did I tell you? You found your dream man." Eden beamed.

"You were right. It's time we found yours." She nudged her side.

"First things first. Let me get settled into my new apartment." Eden grinned.

Mason and Brittany approached.

"Couldn't be happier for you, Gabby." Mason hugged her then turned to Dylan. "You've got one of the best here, don't ever forget it."

"Trust me, I know." Dylan beamed, not taking his eyes off her.

Stu clapped Dylan on the shoulder. "I guess this means you're moving off-site."

"I'll still be on the ranch at the crack of dawn. Don't worry."

"I won't." Stu winked, his toothpick bobbing as he turned to congratulate Gabby.

"We have plenty of time to figure it out." She patted Dylan's chest. Then it hit her—Phoebe would finally have a daddy. A real daddy. The waterworks threatened behind her eyes again, and she had to close them tight for a moment.

"Say, have you two seen Gretchen around?" Stu asked.

"Um, I don't know." Dylan peered through the crowd. "Is that her over there?"

Stu turned and made a beeline to the group of church ladies in the corner.

"Sugar, you've found your Herb." Babs hugged Gabby and kissed both her cheeks. "I'm proud of you. You took a chance."

"Because of you." She squeezed Babs tightly. "I needed your tough love."

"You've got a fine cowboy, Gabby. Something tells me you two have a lifetime of adventures waiting."

"Babs?" She searched for the right words. "Thanks for being my mom away from mom."

"You're like a daughter to me." It was Babs's turn to get teary-eyed. "Oh, now look at me. I'll be right back. My mascara is running."

Stella came over. "Nicole wanted to come, but she's got her hands full with the triplets."

"You knew about this?" Gabby was surprised Stella had been so good about keeping the secret.

"Of course, I knew. Babs threatened to hack off my hair if I spilled a word."

Gabby laughed. "Well, I wouldn't expect Nicole to be here. Tell her I'll stop by to see the babies this weekend sometime."

After everyone congratulated them and dispersed, Gabby picked up the roses, inhaling their aroma again, and then admired her ring.

"I guess it's official." Dylan stared into her eyes.

"You're stuck with me, cowboy."

"I wouldn't have it any other way."

\* \* \* \* \*

Dear Reader,

I hope you enjoyed reading this book. I had so much
fun watching Dylan and Gabby fall in love as they em-
braced their identities in ways they struggled with when
the story began. Dylan falsely tied his identity to his
bank account, and he came to the conclusion he wasn't
worth much without his father's money. He was blind to
his many wonderful qualities, and I'm so glad he could
find his true worth in Rendezvous.

Gabby knew she had trust issues with men—with
good reason!—but as time wore on, she realized she
needed to accept that lasting love did exist. With God's
grace, Gabby was able to accept Dylan's love for what
it was—real, special and worth risking her heart over.

May we all step out of our comfort zones as both of
them did and embrace our invaluable worth as children
of God. Nothing can separate us from His love for us!

I love connecting with readers. Feel free to email me
at jill@jillkemerer.com or write me at P.O. Box 2802,
Whitehouse, Ohio, 43571.

Blessings to you,
*Jill Kemerer*

# COMING NEXT MONTH FROM
## Love Inspired

### Available April 21, 2020

## A SUMMER AMISH COURTSHIP
### by Emma Miller
With her son's misbehavior interrupting classes, Amish widow Abigail Stoltz must join forces with the schoolmaster, Ethan Miller. But as Ethan tutors little Jamie, Abigail can't help but feel drawn to him...even as her son tries to push them apart. Can they find a way to become a forever family?

## AMISH RECKONING
### by Jocelyn McClay
A new client is just what Gail Lapp's horse transportation business needs to survive. But as the single mom works with Amish horse trader Samuel Schrock, she's pulled back into the world she left behind. And returning to her Amish life isn't possible if she wants to keep her secrets...

## THE PRODIGAL COWBOY
### *Mercy Ranch* • by Brenda Minton
After their daughter's adoptive mom passes away and names Colt West and Holly Carter as guardians, Colt's determined to show Holly he isn't the unreliable bachelor she once knew. But as they care for their little girl together, can the cowboy prove he'd make the perfect father...and husband?

## HER HIDDEN HOPE
### *Colorado Grooms* • by Jill Lynn
Intent on reopening a local bed-and-breakfast, Addie Ricci sank all her savings into the project—and now the single mother's in over her head. But her high school sweetheart's back in town and happy to lend a hand. Will Addie's long-kept secret stand in the way of their second chance?

## WINNING BACK HER HEART
### *Wander Canyon* • by Allie Pleiter
When his ex-girlfriend returns to town and hires him to overhaul her family's general store, contractor Bo Carter's determined to keep an emotional distance. But to convince her old boss she's home for good, Toni Redding needs another favor—a pretend romance. Can they keep their fake love from turning real?

## AN ALASKAN TWIN SURPRISE
### *Home to Owl Creek* • by Belle Calhoune
The last person Gabriel Lawson expects to find in town is Rachel Marshall—especially with twin toddlers in tow. Gabriel refuses to risk his heart again on the woman who once left him at the altar years ago. But can they overcome their past to consider a future?

---

**LOOK FOR THESE AND OTHER LOVE INSPIRED BOOKS WHEREVER BOOKS ARE SOLD, INCLUDING MOST BOOKSTORES, SUPERMARKETS, DISCOUNT STORES AND DRUGSTORES.**

LICNM0420